Reaching out, Xander rubbed the pad of his thumb under her eye, further smearing the black streak.

He held up his thumb, showing her the smudge.

"Fine, okay, I have raccoon eyes," she said without a sliver of self-consciousness, her folded arms thrusting up her breasts. "What's your point?"

"Looking like you do, flinching at the most innocent touch from me, you'll doom us both within the day."

"If you want me to start slobbering all over you already, no thanks. I've had a rough day as it is."

"Don't tell me you're already admitting defeat in this arrangement. Did you cry at having to marry the big bad monster Xander Skalas instead of the man you could wrap around your finger? Or did you bawl your eyes out because you might have to put in some actual work to get to that trust fund of yours?"

Her breaths rapid, she tugged at the ends of her hair so roughly that her scalp had to prickle. "Underestimate me at your own peril, Xander."

The Powerful Skalas Twins

Taming Greece's most notorious brothers!

Billionaires Alexandros and Sebastian Skalas are known for the immense power they yield in Greece. But they'll be brought to their knees by the two women who can see past their ultrarich reputations.

When the twin brothers are forced to swap places at the altar, Alexandros will step up as Annika Mackenzie's convenient groom while developing a very *inconvenient* attraction...

Read more in
Saying "I Do" to the Wrong Greek

Three years later, Greek billionaire Sebastian still can't forget his night with Dr. Laila Jaafri. Once reunited, the consequences of their passion will force the playboy to do the unthinkable and claim her!

Read more in
A Twin Revelation to Tame Him

Saying "I Do" to the Wrong Greek

TARA PAMMI

Recycling programs
for this product may
not exist in your area.

ISBN-13: 978-1-335-59339-9

Saying "I Do" to the Wrong Greek

Copyright © 2024 by Tara Pammi

For questions and comments about the quality of this book,
please contact us at CustomerService@Harlequin.com.

TM and ® are trademarks of Harlequin Enterprises ULC.

Harlequin Enterprises ULC
22 Adelaide St. West, 41st Floor
Toronto, Ontario M5H 4E3, Canada
www.Harlequin.com

Printed in Lithuania

MIX
Paper | Supporting
responsible forestry
FSC® C021394

Tara Pammi can't remember a moment when she wasn't lost in a book—especially a romance, which was much more exciting than a mathematics textbook at school. Years later, Tara's wild imagination and love for the written word revealed what she really wanted to do. Now she pairs alpha males who think they know everything with strong women who knock that theory and them off their feet!

Books by Tara Pammi

Harlequin Presents

Returning for His Unknown Son

Billion-Dollar Fairy Tales

Marriage Bargain with Her Brazilian Boss
The Reason for His Wife's Return
An Innocent's Deal with the Devil

Born into Bollywood

Claiming His Bollywood Cinderella
The Surprise Bollywood Baby
The Secret She Kept in Bollywood

Signed, Sealed...Seduced

The Playboy's "I Do" Deal

Visit the Author Profile page
at Harlequin.com for more titles.

CHAPTER ONE

SOMETHING WAS WRONG.

Terribly, horribly wrong in the tableau before Annika Saxena-Mackenzie as she stood at the other end of the altar of the centuries-old church, her arm wound through her stepfather's, her lace-and-tulle designer dress weighing her down.

Her gut, her instincts, her heart knew it before her mind, her rationale, seemed to catch up. Or pin it down.

It wasn't the gorgeous smattering of lilies and night jasmines, scattered about randomly to achieve perfection, that made the church look like it was floating on dreamy white flowers.

It wasn't the suitably awed guests, grateful to be invited to the wedding of the century on the East Coast, staring back at her playing her role perfectly—an heiress worth billions.

It wasn't the string quartet she'd hired after dozens and dozens of auditions and which she'd had flown in specially for this occasion from Vienna.

It wasn't her three young half brothers, who were dressed in matching black suits and trying to behave like perfect gentlemen for their older sister even though they were fidgeting rascals who couldn't sit still for breakfast.

It wasn't the officiant standing at the altar and gazing at her with an affected kindness that had cost her a pretty penny.

The setting of her extravagant, storybook, fairy-tale wedding was perfect.

Her stepfather, Killian, looking down at her with pride and joy, always on her side, always loving her unconditionally, was perfect.

She was looking perfect.

It was the man waiting for her that was the problem.

Her bridegroom.

Something was wrong. Something was different—strange—*about him.*

Ani wondered if she should stop walking, tell Killian that she wasn't feeling well. Or excuse herself for just a minute while she put her finger on it.

It had taken her months of strategic planning and cunning scheming and secret meetings with a lawyer and roping in her accessory with pleas and demands and threats to finally get here. She couldn't back out now. Not until...

And then finally, it came to her, halfway through the torturous walk toward her destination, leaving her rational mind horrorstruck.

He was wrong.

Dizziness overtook her as realization landed, the tight corset of her dress making it hard to breathe.

He'd fooled the crowd and the media outside, the awed guests and her stepfather who'd only met him twice. But not her.

Ani had always been able to tell them apart, even when she'd been a four-year-old, forever chasing after the Skalas teens during long, hot Greek summers, when their father couldn't, much less the media.

When she'd been a teen, it had been a point of pride that she was only one of two people who could tell them apart when they didn't want the world to know: their grandmother, Thea, who'd raised them, and her.

Now Ani knew why her heart was ratcheting so hard in her chest, why her belly rolled the moment she passed the grand archway and caught sight of him standing there.

This was the wrong twin.

This was not Sebastian Skalas, the playboy billionaire/ friend/fellow hell-raiser she'd roped into marrying her after months and months of wearing him down.

This was Alexandros Skalas, the exact opposite of the laid-back, glib charmer that was his twin.

Xander was arrogant, egotistical, ruthless, controlling. The one man who got under her skin with no effort. The one man she'd never been able to win over. The one man who could turn her brilliant plan upside down.

Her stepfather nudged her forward, the weight of his palm at her back, inquiring without letting on. Killian's kindness was a potent reminder that she couldn't turn back on her scheme at this crucial point. Not if Xander was playing along.

But why was Xander here? Had Sebastian talked him into it somehow?

However much they butted heads, Xander and Sebastian loved each other. It was a very contentious, competitive kind of affection, but at the end of the day it was love—a sentiment they both considered a weakness.

Two more steps and Killian would hand her over.

Feeling a helplessness she hated, Ani lifted her chin and

faced reality head-on. In a black tuxedo that hugged his lean, wiry strength, her bridegroom was quintessentially masculine, so effortlessly sensual that it drew her and then repelled her for the power it had over her. The patrician nose, the high forehead, the neatly slicked-back hair and that mouth, with its tiny, infinitesimal scar…everything about him was magnetizing, turning her from her rational plans and hard goals and a strong survivor into a mass of feelings and sensations over which she had no control.

One dark brow rose.

This *was* Xander. And with that raised brow, he was asking her if she was going through with it, taunting her to run away, daring her to admit her fear and turn around.

A soft exhale escaped from her mouth, making the lacy veil flutter.

He seemed to think she had a choice. But she had none— not when it came to saving her family. She needed a husband to take hold of her father's wealth that had been left in trust for her—a stupid, archaic condition imposed by her dear departed father and enforced with casual malice by her stepbrother, Niven.

She'd begged and cajoled Sebastian, threatened and cursed in turns, because he was the one man she could trust to not control her once she had her fortune, to not want even a dime of it. For all he was a charmer and a playboy, Sebastian had a hidden core of integrity that had cemented their friendship for almost two decades.

Maybe Xander was going to pretend he was Sebastian and then Sebastian would come back and they could move forward with all that they'd agreed. Which wasn't really much, since she'd asked so little of him as a husband.

Her thoughts in a whirl, Ani took the last two steps and

smiled beatifically when Killian kissed her cheek and asked her a question with those perpetually kind eyes. And then she was standing in front of the man who, it seemed, had decided to see this through.

And that was what rankled the most: that she had to be saved by Xander.

She was going to kill Sebastian with her own bare hands for leaving her to Xander's ruthless ego! Because if there was one thing that she knew for sure in this maelstrom of confusion, it was that Xander disliked her as much as she disliked him.

Very few things in life made Alexandros Skalas curious.

Most things, and most people in life, were predictable and the few variables that he did encounter, Xander made sure fell into easy, predictable patterns, so he rarely encountered surprises or shocks. At only thirty-four, he had already turned into a crotchety, grumpy sort of man who liked his things, his businesses, his routines, the people around him, and his life just so.

And given that he was a billionaire a hundred times over, he could care and not care as he pleased. Mostly he didn't.

But there had always been one variable, one person, he had never been able to fathom or put into a box or…dammit, control. The last thing sounded wrong because he wasn't a person who usually wanted to control others, especially when they existed on the periphery of his life.

Annika Saxena-Mackenzie was that variable that kept surprising him and shocking him. His grandmother's goddaughter, she had always been a part of Xander's life in one way or another. He repeatedly pushed her to the margins, and yet, she kept taking center stage in his life. First as a cute, chubby toddler who had stolen his grandmama's attention and care from him and Sebastian when they'd needed her more, then as an intrusive, irritating teenager who forever dogged his twin's steps during summers, making him laugh and howl and generally participating in his escapades and egging him on to more. Then in the last few years, by suddenly morphing into one of the most beautiful women he'd ever set eyes on.

As if it wasn't enough that his grandmama was excessively fond of Annika, Sebastian had a firm friendship with her. Over the years, Xander had waited for a break to appear, as it usually did in all of Sebastian's relationships.

It didn't. Again, that annoying variable.

Somehow, Annika and Sebastian's friendship had not only lasted for two decades, but it had resulted in a shocking engagement announcement not four months ago.

If Xander told himself that the engagement didn't bother him one bit it would be a lie.

It *had* bothered him. It had been bothering him for all of one hundred and twenty-eight days and twenty-two hours.

Being the deliberate, strategic, non-impulsive Skalas twin—the only one with a sensible head on his shoulders among his entire demented family—Xander had waited, with growing impatience, to see the engagement crash and burn.

It was impossible to imagine two such people—rich, privileged, petty hell-raisers—living together in peaceful matrimony. It was like mixing two explosive chemicals, and all that would follow was destruction. But his twin had surprised him yet again.

Sebastian had not only kept up appearances, plastering himself to Annika's side at every charity gala and society event, he had also cleaned up his act. There hadn't been any scandalous affairs with ministers' wives, or getting drunk in nightclubs and getting into fights. Basically, for the first time in their lives, Xander hadn't had to clean up a single mess that Sebastian had left behind.

In one of those weak moments that seemed to come up on him after three glasses of whiskey, Xander had wondered if Annika was indeed the magic pill to fix whatever ailed Sebastian. The thought had brought the truth into sharp relief followed by blistering distaste.

He did not want Annika as his sister-in-law.

For all the media reported that he and Sebastian hated each other—and they let that rumor feed itself—whoever Sebastian married would be center stage in Xander's life.

Even that was only half the truth.

Cloaked in the darkness of the night, his usual control blunted by alcohol, Xander had finally admitted the truth to himself: he did not want Sebastian to marry Annika *because he wanted Annika for himself.*

With a confounding depth and breadth. With a fierce, possessive, almost savage force.

He had always wanted her. Even though she'd always been attached at the hip to Sebastian. Even though she'd always preferred his charming, easygoing, funny twin over Xander himself. He'd wanted her even when he didn't understand her sudden metamorphosis from a sunny, painfully awkward teenager to a brazen flirt and shameless thief.

Even when she got herself into scandals that led to two broken engagements, and ran with the wrong crowd, and got up in his face about his grandmother's failing health in the last year. Even when he'd discovered that she was siphoning funds from his grandmama. Even when he'd discovered his mother's favorite sapphire ring had disappeared on one of her summer visits.

He had wanted her when he'd kissed her in the gazebo at his estate, under the cover of dark, at her twenty-first birthday party not two years ago. He wanted her, more than anything he had ever wanted in his life, when she had pressed her lithe body up against him and moaned her eagerness and greed for more.

He'd wanted her when he'd whispered, "I have finally figured out how to make you behave." He'd wanted her when she'd jerked away from him, a flash of vulnerability in her eyes before she faked shock. He'd wanted her when she pressed trembling fingers to her swollen mouth, and claimed she'd mistaken him for Sebastian.

He had wanted her even when she'd lied to his face that if she'd known that it was him, she would never have touched him, much less let him kiss her. He had wanted her when her lies had kept him up all night.

Far too invested, he had waited and waited and waited for the engagement to fall apart. But it had not. Not two months ago, not a month ago, not two weeks ago, not a few days ago.

Imagining his dislike for Annika had brought about his absence at the wedding, his grandmother Thea had read him the riot act about what it meant to be a Skalas. Especially since her frail health forbade her traveling to see her favorite grandson marry the apple of her eye. For reasons only known to her, Annika had to get married here, instead of at their ancestral estate.

Xander couldn't reveal to his grandmama that he'd been planning to attend all along. That while he didn't know how, he was going to do his level best to stop the wedding.

Pining for his twin's wife from a distance was an affliction he refused to be struck down with for the foreseeable future. He wouldn't have stolen her for himself like some uncivilized brute being thrashed around by his desires, but he was absolutely going to make sure the wedding couldn't go ahead.

He simply needed to be sure that Sebastian's heart hadn't been engaged. And he was right. His brother was fond of Annika but nothing more.

Because despite their cruel, tyrannical father's countless attempts to pit them against each other, he and Sebastian did care for each other. It was not a traditional sort of affection, but more of a tolerance of each other's flaws and foibles, an understanding of each other's capacity for cruelty that was rooted in their childhood.

Until yesterday morning, Sebastian had been in a high mood. And then, right after the rehearsal dinner last night, he had vanished.

Xander did not worry about his brother, not then, not now. For all he liked to present himself to the world as a useless, charming playboy who only knew how to spend money and waste himself on the wrong women, Sebastian was razor-sharp and just as ruthless as Xander, only he hid his true nature.

They each had their own ways of rebelling against the tight fist of their cruel father. They'd both survived and, even better, they'd both succeeded in their own ways. If that wasn't a big middle finger raised to Konstantin Skalas, Xander did not know what was.

Within half an hour of his brother disappearing, Xander had received Sebastian's call. And what he had been expecting had come true.

Sebastian was unable to marry Annika the next morning.

Xander did not ask why and Sebastian did not venture an explanation. Only that he was caught up in something he could not get out of, for a while. From the rough impatience in his words, Xander wondered if someone had outplayed his devilish twin.

"So you want me to do your dirty work for you? Tell her that you're dumping her at the altar? Can I wait until tomorrow morning at the church to do it? Let me, Sebastian," he said, letting that cruel thread that they'd both inherited come out to play, "let me have the pleasure of telling Annika that her precious bridegroom isn't coming. This could be your birthday gift to me."

"And I thought you hid your cruelty better, brother."

Xander considered his reaction to the news of his brother absconding: relief and delight and something else—an insidious vein of poison he hadn't known was there. "We each have our weaknesses, Sebastian. You very bravely and publicly delight in yours. I shame and beat mine to death before they become a problem."

His twin, showing uncharacteristic wisdom, remained silent. The empty space and spiraling seconds made Xander turn his words over and over in his head. He wasn't impulsive and yet sometimes, there was freedom in lack of control. In the dark, delicious things that emerged when he wasn't actively suppressing every emotion. Damn his brother.

"What is that you want from me?" he finally asked, incensed with himself. He had clearly not been at his best for this…to become such a problem. Maybe ignoring it instead of tackling it head-on had been the fault.

"Marry Ani tomorrow morning."

Ani... The pet name that fell so easily from his twin's lips worked him up into a lather. The fact that he hadn't immediately refused Sebastian's ridiculous, crazy plan was a fact neither of them missed.

"And why would I do that?" he asked, holding at bay a torrent of images coming at him. When had he ever found himself this badly prepared, this out of touch with a situation, that there were this many revelations?

Never.

And yet, in the case of the unruly heiress, as he called her in his head, he was like a green teenage boy who had no control over his body and what it wanted.

"You and I both know you're actively searching for a bride, Xander."

"No."

"Then how do I know that you terrify half the young, eligible women in society?" Now Sebastian was enjoying this. "They come crying to me after you find them not good enough, after you scare them away with your ridiculous, outdated standards and terrifying expectations. All the business-minded papas want you, Xander, yes, but the young women...it's me they want."

Every word out of his twin's mouth was true and Xander kept quiet. He'd thought he'd successfully hidden from Sebastian his efforts at finding a suitable wife but clearly, he'd been no good at it.

"Poor Xander, tasked with carrying on the great Skalas name and legacy. Cursed to follow in Papa's footsteps and create little pyscho Skalases for the next generation."

"Skalas Bank is a four-hundred-year-old institution that has only ever been headed by a Skalas family member and we kicked out the rotten apple at great personal cost. Why should I give up everything I've worked for so relentlessly since I was sixteen because Grandmama has decided to have a tantrum all of a sudden?"

"Tantrum or not, she's the majority shareholder, Xander. Unless she transfers her shares to you, you will not be named president. Did you know that she's been having clandestine meetings with dear cousin Bruno?"

Xander cursed. Obsessed with this farce of an upcoming wedding, he'd missed that too. Bruno was another rotten apple in the family tree who would raze the bank to ashes if given even a little control. "She's too fond of the family name and the *sacred institution* to let him in."

"Her sisters all have a multitude of grandchildren, Xander. And she just had that heart scare. You're not at your best if you can't see what's going on with her. She hates Bruno just as much as you and I do, which is why this has become a crisis for her. And you know she won't relent. She's like a dog with a bone when she sets her mind to something."

"Be respectful, Sebastian."

His brother laughed again, and Xander was surprised to hear the sound of shackles. Actual metal shackles. Somehow, Xander overcame the impulse to ask Sebastian what the hell was going on with him.

"Oh, I respect the old biddy as much as you do, Xander. If it wasn't for her, God knows where we would have ended up, thanks to our dear psychotic father. She will wear you down until you accept someone of her choice. This way, you are taking proactive action, and you, my dear twin, are the most proactive man I know. And, ta-da, here's a ready-made bride for you. With a shelf life of no more than two years."

"As sweet as your sacrifice is, I intensely dislike the idea of your hand-me-downs."

His brother cursed and Xander wondered at how their roles seemed to have suddenly changed. Where were these pathetic, childish taunts coming from? How resentful had he grown?

"I know you think I planned this but I didn't, Xander. I didn't mean to be…incapable of showing up tomorrow." His tone softened. "I am asking you for a favor. I don't want Ani to be humiliated. And there's more than just humiliation at stake for her. She's my friend, she asked me for help and I'm letting her down."

"She asked you for help?" Suddenly, Xander felt like he had a key to the complex mystery that was Annika Saxena-Mackenzie. He'd never have been attracted to an empty-headed twit and even that…had been a recent development. It wasn't the girl he'd known in her teens.

Sebastian hesitated and it spoke more clearly than if he'd given a straight answer.

"How?" Xander persisted. "If you want me to step into your shoes, you'd better answer my questions."

"Ani asked me."

"Asked you what?"

"To marry her." Before he could pounce another question on him, his twin muttered, "I can't tell you more, Xander. I won't betray her confidence."

"You're asking me to marry a woman who asked *you* to marry her, Sebastian. I've pretended to be you when father's rage was high, but this is too much. Too tacky even for you."

"It's not… Ani and I…it's not a real thing, okay? Just do this. For me. For her."

Xander laughed. "She knows you better than anybody.

Better than even I do, probably. She should've known what she was getting into."

"Damn it, Xander! You're going to let your bruised ego stop you from helping her?"

Xander let out a soft curse. His brother was in fine form today.

Had it bruised his ego that Annika had asked his twin for help instead of him? It angered him even as he understood the unformed, raw emotion: this expectation of being needed by her. And the longer he thought about it, the more it perturbed him. He should walk away now, let her face what she alone had brought on herself. It was the kind of ruthless thinking that had made him who he was today.

Sebastian sighed. "Listen, Xander, I'm not sure how long I can talk for but I made a guess about you and—"

"Enough, Seb," Xander muttered, steel in his voice. He hated being manipulated and his brother knew that better than anyone else on the earth.

"Don't punish her for my games, okay! That's not you, Xander. Don't leave her standing there."

"I'm not handing her back to you when you return."

Sebastian cursed. "What? Listen, Xander! She and I—"

Xander had cut the call then. He didn't want to hear more. What was the point in stretching out the string of weird confidences?

Both he and Sebastian had known that he would step in from the moment he'd asked. Whether he was doing it for his twin or for Annika was a question he refused to speculate on. The third choice was the right answer: he was doing it for himself.

And now here he was, waiting to see if she'd walk the last few steps. Because she knew.

Annika had always known when it was him.

And if she wanted to marry him, if she was that desperate for a husband, then she'd have to acknowledge it was him she was marrying, that he was the one who was rescuing her. He refused to pretend to be anyone else at his own damned wedding.

CHAPTER TWO

ANNIKA THOUGHT SHE'D made her peace with the situation, but she fared no better by the time she stepped up to *him*.

It would help so much to think of him as a placeholder—whatever the reason he was holding his twin's place. It would be so much better if she could view Alexandros Skalas as just any man who was coming to her aid, would help so much if she didn't feel this combination of shuddering relief and begrudging gratitude, and the inexplicable fury that *he* was the one standing there.

And the gut-level conviction that now, with him in charge, everything would be all right. *That* stung her throat like bile.

For all she'd cultivated a persona as an inveterate flirt—an empty-headed, fun-loving, spoilt heiress who jumped from man to man, who had the slight problem of sticky fingers when it came to shiny baubles, who had two broken engagements behind her—it was impossible to continue that act with him.

It had always been impossible to pretend that Alexandros Skalas was any other man that had come into her life's narrow purview. She was used to men and their fragile egos and their petty demands and their near manic need to control her and chain her and bind her and yet it seemed that a lifetime wasn't enough to get used to him.

She was shaking when he lifted her veil.

If she could kick herself right now for going with a traditional lace veil, she would. Because this...unveiling at his hands felt too much like her undoing, the beginning of her unraveling.

A full-body shiver took hold of her. As if her humiliation wasn't complete, it took his large hands gently resting on her bare shoulders for her racing pulse to slow down. Even that—the kindness that her body seemed to crave from him—she hated. It was a betraying weakness, and like a predator, Xander would catalog them all.

She lifted her chin and looked into his eyes.

Once again, she was hit by the striking distinction between the twins. How could everyone not sense the difference in their energies, in their personalities?

Sebastian was all easy charm, smooth smiles and sneaky, dry humor.

This man in front of her was built in a different way on a cellular level. If his brother made his way through life mocking and taunting, and making fun of everything sacred, Xander was the one who made the rules by which most of that Greek society functioned. He was considered to be one of the most ruthless and brilliant bankers in a crumbling economy, held the loyalty of every employee and commanded great respect even among his enemies. And to top it all off, he was extremely private.

He was like this...big, mysterious, magically foolproof treasure box that Annika had always desperately wanted to crack open, especially when she was younger and hadn't taken on the burden of protecting her family from her psycho stepbrother.

With the reckless courage of a young woman believing her own hype, she'd even tried to crack the code of what made Xander tick.

Now, standing there, she was surprised by her own daring. How reckless and self-destructive she had to have been to kiss this man, to lose herself in it, and then pretend that she'd thought all along that it was his twin? She'd been burned by his kiss, and then by his blistering contempt. Only, the scars were invisible, like all the others.

The pad of one thumb climbed up to her bare shoulder and, to her shame, Ani found herself leaning into the touch. Dark gray eyes watched her, and she wondered if there was a laser built into his mind—his eyes on her felt like he was forever probing her.

Once, she'd made the mistake of thinking that it was curiosity that Xander held for her. Because curiosity meant interest, right? And that had led her silly self into thinking it meant her interest—her fascination with him—might be returned.

But Xander had very effectively put paid to that foolish hope, reminding her why she'd always felt such a strange, dangerous awareness near him: it was what prey felt near a camouflaged predator.

He thrived on control. He thrived on order and discipline and that brittle self-sufficiency that made powerful men start to believe in their superiority over everyone else, that made them want to turn people into puppets.

Her stepbrother from her father's second marriage was a control freak too and until Killian had rescued her from him, Ani had barely kept her spirit intact under the boot of his cruelty, which masqueraded as care and concern.

Xander was a thousand times more powerful, more tightly wired, and seemed to hold an infinite capacity for that same casual cruelty. Annika reminded herself of those crystal-clear words she'd heard him say to his grandmother not a year ago.

"I don't understand why you're so fond of that...frivolous, empty-headed twit. Why are you so supportive of her when she can't be loyal to anyone? When she's got nothing to recommend her except a fortune that might never truly be hers? In case you forgot, she stole from you. She stole my mother's ring."

"She's my goddaughter, Xander. And whatever she is, she deserves my care and protection." Thea's defense of her had tears falling down her cheeks. Because even without Ani confiding in her, Thea had known the utter hell she'd been living in back then, before Killian had won custody of her; before she'd been allowed to go live with her stepfather and her three young brothers.

"She's a thief and a flirt and a—"

"Enough, Xander. It is *my* fortune I wish to share with her. Not yours."

"She's a manipulative gold digger, Grandmama. If you can't see that, if you want to lose your money on her, then so be it."

It was exactly the face she'd always presented to the world—this persona that would keep her away from her stepbrother's controlling nature, keen eye and utter greed to take hold of her fortune too.

But she'd expected that Xander would see through her deception, or at least have a little affection for the girl that had once hero-worshipped him. Thea had never asked her to explain her sudden shenanigans and loved her the same. Sebastian had probed gently but retreated when she'd told him that she had to fight her demons herself, that try as she might, she couldn't get used to his support.

Only Xander had written her off. Only Xander had decided, by his damned impossible standards, that she wasn't good enough to even look in the eye.

The slap to her face had come from her own expectations. From her own foolish heart's naive hopes.

She had to remember that. She had to remember that Alexandros Skalas did nothing without expecting something in return and she must brace herself for the price she'd have to pay soon.

But even in this, he made her give her assent. Made her agree that yes, she wanted to court *this* destruction—that she wanted to marry him—instead of the kind that awaited her if he walked away.

Annika gave him her answer with a slight tilt of her chin. The horde of captivated guests would love to see her fall apart, and she had no doubt that her stepbrother had planted his spies everywhere.

And she was damned if she would let him win, damned if she would let down the only man who had ever been kind to her.

To remind herself what was at stake, she cast a quick sideways glance to that first row where Killian and her three half brothers were sitting, watching her with pride and joy and love. Xander's brow tied into a tiny scowl as he caught the quick exchange.

She somehow got through the beginning of the service,

feeling nothing but contempt for an institution that had made a prisoner of her mother before she'd met Killian.

Suddenly, the pitch of the priest's tone changed and she was startled, coming out of her trance. She could hear soft, buzzing gasps behind her as if a whole hive of bees had been released, like a cresting wave reaching its peak. Something knotted hard in her stomach and she knew she wasn't going to like this new development. The priest seemed to recover and addressed her bridegroom again.

"Sebastian Skalas, do you take this woman, Annika Saxena-Mackenzie, as—"

"It is *Alexandros* Skalas. If I have to repeat myself one more time..."

Sharp color rose in Xander's cheeks and her breath was stuck somewhere in her lungs as Annika tried not to look like a gaping fish. But her instinctive, almost visceral horror at his words couldn't be arrested or hidden. She turned her face toward him, aware that her body language, every nuance on her face, even the polite tilt of her eyebrows was being noted, and captured, and would immediately be dissected.

The uncaring beast at her side raised his brows and his mouth twitched. It might have been a smile but who knew if Xander Skalas ever smiled? Could one tell when a great fire-spewing dragon was smiling and when it was baring its fangs at you?

Once again, his fingers landed on her cheek, featherlight. She was aware of the silkiness of her own skin by the abrasive pads of his fingers. Another distinction, another separation that only she knew about. Another small but intimate detail that Annika wished she could delete from her brain.

For the entire world watching them, it would look like a lover's tender gesture.

Only Annika knew the truth. He had declared himself to be Alexandros Skalas, and if she was not in agreement, he would walk away.

It was a laying down of terms, she realized, all those little shivers having returned to dance across her body. He was telling her that this was how it would be if she wanted him as a husband.

How Annika wished she could scream in his face! She didn't want to want him. She just needed a husband for two years in order to beat her abusive brother at his own game.

But whatever it was that Sebastian had told Xander, it was clear that he would only do it on his terms.

Take it or leave it, his eyes said, watching her with that intensity that had always made her feel like a pinned butterfly. A butterfly whose colors were all false camouflage and who beneath it all was nothing but a scared, flawed, maybe even a broken, bird.

She turned away from him, from his touch, making sure to paste on a wide smile that could be caught in the periphery just before she did. The priest repeated his question, and Xander said yes.

Then that booming voice turned to her. "Annika Saxena-Mackenzie, do you take this man, Alexandros Skalas, to be your wedded husband?"

Annika's hurried affirmative cut off the priest and a gurgle of laughter broke out behind her.

Already, she could feel the crowd lapping up whatever it was that Xander served. Even she could see the draw of him despite being a reluctant pawn he was moving about on the board that she'd thought was under her control.

This was Alexandros Skalas, a man who found fault with everything and everyone. A man who conducted his affairs—all kinds of affairs—with utmost privacy. The man who, in contrast to his twin who shockingly revealed every *passage* of his life, played his cards very close to his heart. And she knew what the narrative would look like.

Here was Xander Skalas, in his twin's place, a victor once again, having maneuvered his twin's fiancée into being his wife instead.

As if her waking nightmare wasn't entertaining enough, Xander bent down from his great height and nudged her shoulder with his. It was such a playful, completely uncharacteristic move from him that she looked up.

"I would prefer your 'yes' a little louder, *yineka mou*. We do not want our guests to think that this was a shock to you too, do we?"

"What?" she said, the single word vibrating with a belligerence that she could not quite control. A long time ago, Annika had decided that her wedding was going to be a farce. But she'd never imagined that it would come about with such brutal reality and in such Technicolor, because what was this if not a farce of the worst kind?

His gray eyes gleamed. "As appetizing and juicy as all this gossip would be to Sebastian, *I* do not wish to be known as the man who stole his twin's bride. So I suggest that whatever your reason for acting out this farce, you had better do it with a lot more enthusiasm than you're showing. I would prefer not to be a source of gossip at my own wedding."

"And how is that my fault?" she whispered, regretting the words the minute she said them. Like it or not, Xander was saving her hide, giving her a chance to save her entire family. She could not afford to annoy him.

She faced the priest and declared in her usual naive, blundering way that yes, she would very much like to and was quite eager to marry Alexandros Skalas.

And then it was over and she wanted to rip the stupid veil off her head and tear the dress from her body so she could breathe. Months of planning and sneaking about, and riveting herself to Sebastian's side in tacky, public displays of affection… All of her act had reached its ending.

"You may now kiss the bride," the priest announced, as if he were the avenging angel come to make sure every one of her punishments was meted out.

"Shall I, *matia mou*?" Xander asked, the perfect gentleman.

If she said no, he wouldn't touch her. She knew that. But if she said no, her farce wouldn't be complete. And the worst part was that she wanted to say yes. She wanted to use the occasion to fulfill her darkest wish.

She nodded, unable to voice her assent.

Something dark glittered in his eyes as his long fingers circled her nape, and then she was being kissed to within an inch of her life. It was such a skillful kiss that it made her forget to breathe within two seconds. It was also an assault.

A call to arms.

A declaration of war.

It was also revenge for how she'd taunted him after that kiss all those years ago. Revenge for how she'd blatantly lied that she had mistaken him for Sebastian.

Stars exploded behind her eyes and Ani clutched him, afraid she'd fly away if she didn't. His mouth was rough and firm, and when she gasped, he stole into her mouth, ravishing her very will away from her.

It was the right kiss, the best kiss she'd ever had, and she'd kissed enough men to know that. But for all the wrong reasons.

It made her breath flutter about all over her body like a butterfly. It made her rise to her toes and sink into him, forgetting all her inhibitions, forgetting that this was a man she shouldn't kiss with such eager greed. It was a kiss that made a mockery of the months of worrying and fears and doubts that she wouldn't be able to protect her family. Everything misted away under the onslaught of his firm lips and wicked tongue and utter control of her.

There was pleasure in giving up control, Annika thought then, clinging to his tall, lean, firm body like a puppet, in surrender to someone who'd take away her will, yes, but also her worries.

And suddenly the tenor of the kiss shifted from an assault to something tender and infinitely sweeter and achingly perfect. Her heart thudded against her rib cage. One hand clasped her cheek while the other stroked over her back, gentling her. Now she was the one nipping and chasing and demanding and…

It was the tenderness that broke her. It was always the tenderness that broke her and reminded her that she was being a needy, naive fool once again.

She, who had molded herself, who had trained herself to expect only cruelty in this life. Tenderness was not to be trusted, not to be welcomed and definitely not to be reveled in, as she was doing now, drinking it up like a fool who didn't know the bitter taste of hope.

It was a habit Killian had tried to break her of but she wasn't sure if she would ever be separated from it.

And suddenly, she hated Xander with a surge of fury fueled by old wounds, for making the kiss into something they both knew wasn't true. She'd take his raised brows and twitching mouth and silky threats over false sweetness.

She broke away from the kiss, but before she did, she bit his lower lip. Hard. His fingers tightened over her back and his hips—that had maintained a respectable distance until then—chased hers and for a second, Annika felt the shocking, scalding weight and shape of his erection against her lower belly. An action and its reaction. For a second, just for a second, she wasn't sure if she had the strength to pull back.

She did, by sheer force of will.

On instinct she couldn't fight at a conscious level, she hid her face in his chest.

Nothing like running toward the storm that was determined to drown you, she thought, and still, she couldn't detach from the solid, hard haven his chest offered. At least she'd look like a blushing bride hiding her tremulous smiles and swollen lips and scalding arousal from the world. Like she'd been cajoled into a sweet kiss instead of being ravished into surrender.

CHAPTER THREE

ANNIKA RUSHED INTO the bridal suite that her stepfather had booked for her as a treat—something he couldn't afford—escaping the already short reception that she and Sebastian had planned to the last minute.

Since his reputation was that he was unconventional, he'd have it put about that he was eager to get away with his gorgeous bride before they had to show up at the Skalas mansion in Greece. And she, not only needing a breather from the circus act she'd put on for the last few months, but also to visit Thea, had agreed readily.

Being introduced to the very extensive and very greedy Skalas family by the matriarch Thea was a rite every new bride must get through, Sebastian had announced loudly when Niven had been about to invite her and Sebastian to his own estate in the Hamptons.

She had no doubt that Niven would use the flimsiest excuse he could find to deny Ani access to her trust fund. She knew the extreme necessity of showing to the world that her marriage was very much a match for the ages. It was imperative that she and her husband reflect matrimonial bliss.

And yet, she hadn't been able to stand next to Xander and pretend that she was a blissfully-in-love bride. If she had to take his beatific smile any longer or dance with him or eat a piece of cake from his bare fingers one more time, she'd explode. Or was it implode with her own desires?

Somehow, she'd managed to evade Killian. Either she'd burst into tears or admit to the whole farce. She needed a moment to think, to catch her breath, to not be drowned in the scent of a man she couldn't resist and couldn't trust.

What had felt like a cunning farce with Sebastian now felt all too real. As if to remind her, the beautiful princess-cut diamond and the simple platinum band felt unbearably heavy on her finger.

With a soundless scream, she tugged the veil off roughly, uncaring that pins went flying and she was plucking her hair out by the roots. She kicked off her heels, and was twisting herself inside out to get to the hundreds of tiny eyelet buttons studded with pearls at the back when the doors to the suite opened. She stilled, wondering if Xander knew he was playing with a cornered feral animal who would bite, kick and fight for what was hers.

Xander tucked his hands into his trouser pockets and eyed the rabid chaos of the suite. Makeup tubes and pots, designer handbags, at least ten pairs of heels strewn about, expensive lingerie, and a pile of unopened gifts on every surface...his new wife stood in the eye of a storm, her expression a heady combination of outrage and helplessness.

Then there was the way the lace of the dress kissed her bare shoulders and gleaming, golden-brown skin. Slender shoulders and a tiny frame, with lush curves in between. The flimsy fabric clung to her breasts and her hips, somehow bringing out all of that elegant voluptuousness into striking relief. Her dark golden hair fell in thick waves, the ends grazing her breasts.

In a nervous gesture he remembered from when she'd been all gawky limbs, her fingers played with the dark ends. Even that served to heighten his awareness of her as the movement flashed her ring finger at him.

Satisfaction swirled through him when he'd caught her surprise in the moment he'd removed Sebastian's ring—a gaudy, flashy diamond—and replaced it with an elegant sapphire sitting amid a cluster of tiny diamonds. For a man whose only example of marriage had been the disastrous one between his abusive father and his alcoholic mother, he felt quite the possessive rush at seeing her branded with jewelry he'd personally picked.

Branded...

Imagining her outrage at the term made the high he was riding even sweeter. *She was his...*for as long as she needed him. For as long as they needed to work each other out of their systems.

Because for all her lies and playacting—and he was beginning to realize the real Annika was buried beneath a heap of it—she wanted him. That kiss had betrayed both of them. Christos, he'd never been revved up so fast.

Whatever her reason for asking Sebastian to marry her, he would see it through. Being a natural and brilliant problem solver, he could present her with a solution that was a thousand times better than anything Sebastian could have cobbled together. Now he just had to convince his prickly bride that he'd done her a favor.

"What are you doing here?" she asked, tilting her chin up.

She was the sexiest woman he'd ever met and yet, Xander knew without doubt, it was her spirit that provoked his baser instincts, her spirit he wanted to conquer. He wondered if Konstantin's madness had been passed on to him, despite his every effort not to be the cruel monster his father had been.

"You escaped the reception without your usual flair for drama. I thought it a good idea to follow since we want to create the impression that I can't keep away from my… luscious bride. Especially after saving her from the horrible fate of being left at the altar."

"I didn't ask to be saved by you, Xander. I'd rather—"

"An annulment won't be that hard to achieve, then," he said smoothly, flashing his cell phone at her. "Shall I call my lawyer?"

"No, wait!" Her chest rose and fell with a long inhale of air and a boatload of pride, no doubt, which had always been like a live flame. "I need this marriage. And I…appreciate you stepping in."

"Glad you didn't choke on that."

Her eyes gleamed with challenge. "I guess that's one thing you can provide better than Sebastian—brutal honesty."

"You know very well that there are a lot of things I can do better than my rascal twin."

The pulse at her neck fluttered like a trapped butterfly's wings as she bit out, "That's…a disgusting thing to say."

"I'm a better financial provider, better at sticking to commitments, better at giving you security. Why, dear wife, which scandalous place did your mind go to?"

Pink dusted her cheeks as she resolutely held his gaze. "Point to Alexandros Skalas. But you'd better remember I'm not a wind-up toy you stole from Sebastian because you suddenly decided you fancy it."

"Let's not moralize to each other, Annika. After all, you

thought nothing of lusting after one brother and scheming to marry the other."

She flinched but recovered with a refreshing verve he found in very few adversaries. Was that her appeal? Most women were intimidated by him, his standards, his demands. Annika's stubbornness, willfulness and recklessness, on the other hand, seemed to grow inversely at his censure.

A dangerous smile wreathed her lips. "How do you know I don't lust after you both? Or that I don't consider you interchangeable? Or that I don't care whose bed I hop into or whose ring I wear as long as I reach my destination?"

Ugly jealousy such as he'd never known before struck Xander like a punch to his solar plexus. There was no earthly reason for him to be jealous of his twin, he who'd borne the brunt of their cruel father's brutality growing up, who hid his scars even from his brother. It wasn't that he considered himself superior to Sebastian—they just had different personalities and different priorities. They went about beating their demons into submission in different ways. And somehow his had led him to...the woman staring at him, challenge pouring out of every delicious inch of her. The awareness that she very much knew the competitive streak and its origins between him and Sebastian and still chose to deploy it as a tactic didn't dim the effect one bit.

He wanted to be the victor with her, even when he didn't know what the spoils were.

He swallowed down the dark, unwieldy jealousy coating his throat. Taking her bait was beneath him, especially when she was only responding to his provocation. "Point to Annika Skalas," he said, going for a soft thrust.

It struck harder and truer than he'd expected because

her entire body seemed to bow and bend. "Actually, strike that," she said, rubbing a hand over her face wearily. "I wanted Sebastian. I chose Sebastian. I…needed Sebastian. But when has life ever been fair, right? So I'll make do with you."

"I'm sure it's extra frustrating because you can't manipulate me like you do Grandmama and Sebastian. Grandmama, I still see it, but Sebastian…he's never struck me as gullible."

"At least I'm aware of the shallowness of my life, Xander, that I'm willing to do whatever it takes. You, on the other hand, sit on your high horse, sneering down at us. You forget that I know you. You didn't do this out of the goodness of your heart. So please, enough of this mudslinging. I thought, with you, we could get down to business without catering to your masculine ego. Or am I mistaken in that too?"

"How refreshing, Annika," Xander said, honest for once. In all his search for a potential bride, he hadn't met one woman half as gutsy or half as honest. Or half as self-aware, he added to himself. Again, the disparity between the image she presented and the real woman was disarming. "What are your requirements?"

"I need this marriage to last at least a year. I need my stepbrother to believe that we're the very definition of matrimonial bliss. I need you to blatantly advertise your abiding love and loyalty to me at every public opportunity so that the antiquated conditions my father set in the will are met."

"And what does that get you?" he asked, showing his apparent distaste for the sort of PDA in which his twin specialized.

"My trust fund," she said unflinchingly. "My father, for

some godforsaken reason, decided to appoint his stepson, Niven Shah, as the trustee."

"This is the stepbrother Killian Mackenzie fought for custody of you?" Thea had mentioned that Annika was caught in a custody battle between her dead father's stepson and her stepfather, Killian. After years, Killian had won. "Didn't Killian know he wouldn't be getting his hands on your fortune?"

Rage licked into her eyes and her voice went low. Her face was a map of her loyalties, her dreams. "Killian has no—"

She breathed in deeply, and he could see her picking up the shards of her armor and putting them back in place.

"This is about me and my money. I'm sick of living on handouts from Thea, Killian and even Sebastian. Sick of having to watch every penny, of living in a crummy house with my three half brothers, sick of shopping at discount stores. I want the life I was born to."

"Today's wedding was anything but cheap."

"Sebastian paid for it," she said with that careless shrug. "I want a carefree, easy, luxurious lifestyle and it is my birthright, just as the Skalas throne is yours."

"My right to the Skalas throne has been won through almost two decades of hard work. Or there would only have been rubble to sit on."

"Oh, and my right to my father's wealth is unearned?" Anguish flared in those gorgeous eyes, then disappeared in a flash, making him wonder if he'd imagined it. "Enough games, Xander," she said, sounding exhausted. "Why did you show up? I'd think seeing me humiliated would have been your greatest joy."

"The idea of you owing me a favor was too delicious to pass up."

"You don't do kindness. You don't do anything for your own pleasure even. *Why did you step in?*"

He stared at her and wondered at how well she knew him, and at the shrewdness with which she parried words. There was more to her than the empty-headed, grasping, greedy woman he'd thought her. "I need a wife, just as you need a husband."

She laughed then, a genuine thousand-watt smile on her face that made every inch of her light up. The sound was... husky and arousing and magnetic. His head felt as if he was suddenly swimming in blinding sunshine, the sensation both pleasurable and painful. Her body undulated with her laughter, a shimmering, sensual vision in white whose layers he wanted to peel back one by one.

"This is too good. Are you telling me the hot, brooding, ruthless billionaire banker Alexandros Skalas couldn't find a woman to marry him? Is Sebastian really unavailable or did you have a hand in detaining him so that you could swoop in and steal me?"

What would she do if she knew how close she was to the vague plan in the back of his head if Sebastian hadn't called him? "I find pale, quivering, half-terrified women with zero wit loathsome and boring. My requirements, if you must know, are few, the most important being that I should at least get an intelligent reply back in a conversation."

Her eyes widened, that pink cresting her cheeks again. He had the most insane urge to lick her up, as if it were hot summer and she the cold drink that would satiate his thirst. *The only drink.* "You've got to be joking."

"That's Sebastian's arena, *ne*, and apparently that inane

humor of his is what makes him popular. I can count on one hand the number of women, and men, who will look me in the eye. Even fewer who stand up to me. Who challenge me. Who provoke me." *Who make me lose control.* "The hunt for a bride became as taxing as pretending to like all my various greedy cousins."

She swallowed and he thought she understood what drew him to her. What had always drawn him to her, even when he loathed her for having no integrity or standards or… boundaries.

Looking down, she tugged at the lace on her sleeve. "Here I thought you'd want a biddable wife, Xander. Someone who follows your instructions from dawn to dusk without question. Someone you can review and rate based on pedigree and performance, someone who would bend and bow to satisfy your robotic need for control."

"Where is the challenge with someone who's already cowering and admitting defeat?" he said silkily, and had the reward of seeing her breasts rise and fall. What he wouldn't give to have her beg him to rip that dress off her, to turn all of that aggression and animosity into passion, to have her on her knees, giving him her surrender. What he wouldn't give her in return. "It's gratifying to know you've thought, at length, about my preferences in a wife, *yineka mou*."

"It's not like I have to sit and think about it. You're just so infuriating and calculating that—"

He raised a brow and waited.

"Oh, go to hell!" she bit out. She rubbed long fingers over her temple. "Two hours of being married to you and I already have a headache."

"I, on the other hand, am already enjoying the state of

matrimony. Grandmama is right. The right partner makes all the difference."

She cursed. Long and colorfully. Grabbing a water bottle, she chugged half and poured half over her head. Like her, nothing could contain her unruly hair, and most of the water pooled down over her impressive chest. Her nipples jutted against the lace and lust hit him hard. If she'd done it on purpose, he'd have reacted. With the mascara running down her sunken cheeks, he knew she was exhausted.

"Grandmama refuses to pass on the presidency of Skalas Bank to me if I don't marry."

Annika frowned, tension bracketing her lush mouth. "Thea expects your marriage to be fruitful. She wants heirs for the Skalas legacy, not some ridiculous farce of a wedding."

"That's not on offer, then?" he said, unable to resist the taunt. "I haven't been through the Ts & Cs yet."

"What, sleep with you *and* give birth to little Skalas devils like you?" she scoffed. "No thanks. I want a free, easy life. Not one of obligation and duties."

"It would be anything but obligation between us."

"I'm not attracted to you, Xander."

"Are you trying to convince me or yourself?"

"I'm not. And even if I were, I wouldn't act on it. For all the trust funds in the world."

"And yet I'm sure your prenup with Sebastian—"

"We didn't sign one."

He stilled. So much was at stake and Sebastian did this? "My brother is many things but he's not foolish."

"Something we agree on finally."

"Then why?"

"It's unfathomable to you, isn't it? Sebastian trusts me."

"It's sheer foolishness."

"Forget Sebastian. I'm stuck with you and, believe me, I'd beg on the streets before I take a penny from you."

"This marriage is becoming more and more interesting by the minute, Annika. A year, then. You behave as the perfect, doting wife, and convince Thea—"

For the first time that day—or ever—she looked defeated. "I don't think you've thought this through. I can fool any number of people, the entire damned world, but not Thea. She knows me too well."

"And despite that, she's inordinately fond of you. I've never understood it. She was elated that her favorite outrageous grandson was marrying you. That you'll truly be part of the family now. That she'll never have to part from you." It was only as he said it that Xander wondered how his grandmother would react to the news that he had married her precious goddaughter.

It wouldn't be favorable, but he would overcome her anger as he did everything else.

"By that very same logic, she'll find it impossible to believe that this isn't a farce," Annika argued. "She knows you and I hate each other's guts. She knows I'd never give up on my dream by tying myself to you."

"I thought I was bringing your dreams to fruition, Annika. Is this a different dream?" When she glared at him, he raised his palms. Something about riling her was incredibly energizing, as if he were a device finally thrust into its charging port.

"Thea understands lust, attraction, desire. She'll believe that our mutual hate boiled over into more when necessity struck. We will tell her I was overcome by tenderness for you when I learnt that Sebastian was ditching you at the last minute. Despite the dragon she likes to pretend she is, Thea loves a grand love story."

"Tenderness? You?"

"As believable as loyalty in you."

"I don't like the idea of cheating Thea."

"And what has your entire life been so far?"

"Fine. Fine! I'll slobber all over you and you can pretend as if taking care of me is your greatest wish in life. Just so you know, Niven's…a controlling bastard. He'll try a lot of things to cheat me out of what's rightfully mine. He'll fill your head with any number of disgusting lies about me. He'll do everything he can to make you hate me."

The fear and bitterness in her eyes when she spoke of her stepbrother made Xander's stomach churn. He hated nothing more than a bully picking on weaker people. Why hadn't he ever heard her speak of this man? What was he missing?

"He doesn't know that that my opinion of you can't get any lower," he said, wanting to see her fighting spirit back.

"No, he doesn't," she said, relief shuddering in a long exhale. "That's the one thing to my advantage. He will be a small predator being stalked by a bigger, badder one."

"You think your stepbrother and I are alike?" Xander said, holding his shock back by the skin of his teeth. Did she think him a monster? Did he care? How deep had she dug her hooks into him already?

"Niven's domineering, ruthless, and pounces on others' weaknesses. He thrives on asserting his reach and power. You are a step ahead because you control your own weaknesses with just as much resolve. So, yes, I guess if anyone can take him on, it's you."

"Is that gratitude I hear?"

She glared at him just as a loud knock sounded at the door to the suite, followed by the voices of quarreling boys. "That's my brothers and Killian. Give me half an hour with them and I'll be ready to leave."

Ignoring the chaos she'd created, he ventured farther into the suite, closer to her. With every step he took, she stiffened until he could very well believe that she was a statue. "I'd like to meet them."

"No."

"You've only made me curious."

"Fine. I hope my brothers rub their sticky, chocolate-covered fingers all over your Armani suit."

Xander donned his poker face, even though the picture she painted urged him to leave. How did she know that he was...allergic to children? That whatever legacy Thea wanted would be provided by one of Sebastian's very probably illegitimate children born out of one of his numerous affairs?

"I hope the little one crawls into your lap and barfs in your face," she continued, fascinatingly bloodthirsty. "And the middle one collects worms and ants and bugs and—"

"*Ani? Ani!* Let us in. We want to see you," came a small boy's voice.

"Is it true you married Sebastian's twin?" came another. "I heard someone say he's not fun or cool like Seb. Why'd you have to go and marry him?"

"Ayush Mackenzie, watch your language!" came Killian Mackenzie's gruff voice.

"That's what everyone's saying, Dad," said a fourth voice, almost on the cusp of manhood. This one was truly worried about his sister, painting a different picture than the one Xander had anticipated. "They said Ani's new husband is a horrible, monstrous bully. We can't let her go with him. If he hurts Ani, I'll try my right hook on him. I've gotten really good."

Holding up the train of her dress, a triumphant light in her eyes, his new bride moved to the doors and made a bow. "Your wish is my command, Xander. Here's my family."

CHAPTER FOUR

THE FIRST THING Xander noticed when Annika got on the flight—joining him at the private airstrip a whole ninety minutes later than she'd promised—was that her eyes were swollen and red-rimmed, as if she'd spent the entire three hours after he'd left her to her family sobbing her heart out.

The sight was one he disliked intensely. Even worse was an overwhelming need to…fix it. To fix her. He'd never seen her cry—not even when her mother died.

Frowning, he watched her as she slid into her seat as if her limbs were incapable of independent motion. She was still in her wedding dress, which not only had a tear in the hem but was now wrinkled so thoroughly that it looked like she'd rolled around on the floor—which she probably had, with her brothers. Her hair was a mess and she had dark streaks of mascara smudged under her eyes. She should have looked like a failed participant on one of those horrible survivor-type reality shows that his grandmama was forever watching.

Instead, she looked like a beautiful broken bird that Sebastian had once nursed back to life with a tenderness and conviction that Xander had thoroughly envied because he lacked those qualities himself. He felt the same lack now and resented her for making him aware of it.

The flight attendant announced they were taking off. Unmoving, Annika stared out at the private airstrip, a strange melancholy seeming to take hold of her limbs.

Leaning across the table that separated them, Xander pulled the seat belt across her torso and clicked it into place with a rough jerk that he hoped would startle her out of that fugue. She didn't even blink those long lashes. His muscles tightened at the sweet lemon scent of her filling his nostrils.

"Annika, are you ill?"

Her response was a long, shuddering breath, before she turned away and closed her eyes.

He searched for and discarded words to rile her out of it and found himself without a strategy for the first time in his life. In profile, she looked defeated, and he hated seeing that. He wanted a functioning wife, not some delicate creature he had to console. That was the only reason her melancholy was getting to him.

"You look as though you've been dragged through a bush," he said, filling his words with as much contempt as possible. "Or was it a tussle in the bridal suite with one of your forlorn exes? Should I not have left you alone for so long?"

"How dare you?" she gritted out.

"Your history gives me the daring. You have three broken engagements behind you, the reason for each more colorful and scandalous than the previous. I might wonder if you've already broken your marital vows and—"

"Of course I didn't, you...*beast*." She fairly spat at the words at him.

"Was that the appeal for Sebastian? That you're without morals or boundaries and yet you're honest about all of your vices?"

Like a doll who was being pulled by invisible strings, she flicked those intense eyes open and glared at him. But he didn't miss the red tint flushing her cheeks. "Leave me alone, Xander."

"I'm afraid we haven't reached that stage of marriage yet, as much as we both wish to be there." Reaching out, he rubbed the pad of his thumb under her eye, further smearing the black streak.

She stiffened so visibly that satisfaction swirled through him. He couldn't wait for the day when she'd sink into his touch, or even invite it. He'd never looked forward to something like that.

He held up his thumb, showing her the smudge.

"Okay, I have raccoon eyes," she said without a sliver of self-consciousness, her folded arms thrusting up her breasts. "What's your point?"

"Looking like you do, flinching at the most innocent touch from me, you'll doom us both within the day. Thea might turn vengeful if she smokes us out."

"If you want me to start slobbering all over you already, no thanks. I've had a rough day as it is."

"And what is the reason for that?" he asked casually, using every weapon in his arsenal to incite her into betraying herself.

"Like I'd tell you." Then she looked at him. "Even if I did, you wouldn't get it."

"Don't tell me you're already admitting defeat in this arrangement. Did you cry at having to marry the big bad monster Alexandros Skalas instead of the man you could wrap around your finger? Or did you bawl your eyes out because you might have to put in some actual work to get to that trust fund of yours?"

Her breaths rapid, she tugged roughly at the ends of her hair. "Underestimate me at your own peril, Xander."

She would not reveal the distress he'd seen in her eyes to him, then. Defeat was a bitter pill in his throat.

"Anyway—" her fingers played with the lace cuff of her sleeve, betraying her nervousness "—we're in your private jet. And I have no doubt your lackeys won't betray you to Thea or the media with a single breath."

"True. But I'm not confident in your acting skills, Annika."

"What does that mean?"

"While Sebastian would have gone along merrily with an empty-headed party girl for his wife, I won't. You're married to the chairman of the world's richest, most prestigious bank."

"You haven't been named yet," she said with a gleeful smile, her bare toe grazing his trouser-clad leg in a childish move that both annoyed and pleased him because his tactic had worked.

"And banks and financial institutions," he continued, as if she hadn't interrupted him, "if you didn't know this already, are traditional structures with conservative values. Which is why they'd never accept Sebastian."

"Yes, but don't forget I know Thea as well as you do and she knows me. If I let you make me over into some elegantly boring, mind-numbingly perfect trophy wife, she won't buy it."

"It's a balancing act, then, *ne*?" he said, feeling more alive than he had in years. It was exhilarating to match wit and words with her. "But you might be finally coming up against the one thing Grandmama holds dear, even dearer than you and Sebastian—the Skalas name and legacy. She'll hate you if you taint it with even a small scandal. Better if we lay down some ground rules."

"You mean you'll lay them down and I'll have to follow like a good little soldier?"

"But this is quid pro quo, *ne*?"

"I can't wait to order you around, then," she said, her eyes gleaming with sudden cunning. "Let's get this clear— you'll act the way I want when it's my turn to show you off?"

"I'll be the big bad wolf and huff and puff at your step-brother if you want me to."

A smile touched the corners of her mouth but not her eyes. And he felt a weird sense of defeat.

"A new wardrobe first."

She shook her head, working herself into a temper. That excited Xander more than another woman's mouth on his most responsive parts. Maybe there was something to indulging one's deepest desires like his twin did. To an extent, at least.

"You have a problem with how I dress? Even you can't be such an uptight, controlling—"

"I have an image to maintain in the banking world and you're part of that now," he interrupted calmly. "None of your boho gowns, and tank tops without bras, and shorts with half your ass hanging out and definitely no—"

She straightened with a jerk. "How long have you been waiting to say that to me?"

"No getting drunk and passing out on someone's couch—"

"I didn't realize what a trip this marriage is going to be for you."

"No meetings with shady exes and definitely no stealing from distinguished guests. That is a complete deal-breaker."

She turned red, her jaw working. Then she swallowed. "What if I—"

"Whatever you need, I can provide it, Annika. As my wife, you'll have access to luxuries you've never imagined."

"And if I can't help myself? What then? Will you return me with the price tag attached? Will you get me fixed so that I can work as you intend for me to?"

"If you need medical help, then you'll get it. But that's not the issue, is it?"

Something about his tone made her go still. She licked her lips. "What...do you mean?"

"It's not a compulsion, I know that much. You do it for some other reason. I used to think it was simple greed. But I'm not—"

"I've had enough of you."

He moved his legs so that she was caught between the seat and him. "You embarrass me in any way in front of the world and become a liability instead of an asset, Annika, and I'll make sure you never see a single cent of your trust fund. And we both know it's very much in my power to do so."

Rage shimmered in her eyes. He waited for the explosion, for her temper to fracture like it used to when her mother had been alive. Instead, like a black hole, she swallowed it all back and tucked it away, though where he had no idea. It was horrific to watch her pull everything inward. And it reminded him of...himself, a long time ago. His heart thumped, with excitement at the mystery she presented and also with a niggling sense of dread.

Slowly, she uncoiled from her seat to her full height.

She even managed a smile as she leaned over him, her hands on the armrests, her wide, lush mouth inching closer and closer. Her fingers touched his lower lip, then trailed down to his throat and the V of his shirt. "If I run my finger down, down, down, will I find you hard, Xander?" Her arms pressed her breasts together into a cleavage as she molded her body into a parody of that shallow sensuality most men fell for. Until last night, when he couldn't sleep for wondering how to stop the wedding, he'd been one of that number.

"This is foreplay for you, isn't it? Threatening what someone else holds dear?"

Xander stared into her eyes, and while she could fake the smile and the languid sensuality and the taunting words, her eyes betrayed her. This close, he could see the entire spectrum of emotions there and the most prominent was fear. And as hard as her nearness got him, it was also like being doused in ice-cold water. "Find out for yourself," he said, calling her bluff, hating himself a little in the moment, for even now he could not show her weakness or mercy, not until she had unraveled completely beneath him. "After all, this is supposed to be our wedding night, *ne*?"

Fire burned in her gaze and she moved her palm down his chest to his abdomen, and further down until the base of her palm rested right above his pubic bone. He arrested her fingers.

There was no relief in her eyes, only stubborn determination. "Why stop me when I'm playing right into your hands?"

"Because you're sullying yourself and me, Annika. Because I want your surrender, not your defeat."

Her mouth flinched, and she pulled away as if burnt. A shuddering exhale left her trembling. "Dress me however you want, parade me like a puppet whose strings you're pulling, mold me into a blow-up doll for all I care, but I'll never surrender to you, Alexandros Skalas."

With a growl, she pushed past his legs and stormed into the rear cabin like a furious wraith.

Xander rubbed a hand over his face, feeling as if he'd won the battle but had made a major blunder in the strategy for the war. Clearly, Annika's armor had a breaking point and he'd pushed her past it.

She'd turned the tables on him as only a worthy adversary would. And yet, he didn't like the taste of her pain in his mouth. A part of him wanted to do what she'd suggested— get an annulment and leave her to whatever fate befell her.

Only a small part, however.

The survivor in him recognized the same quality in her. She enticed him no end. The one thing Annika didn't know was how much he thrived on a challenge. How his best came out when the worst was thrown at him.

His father had tried to destroy him before he'd reached his majority, tried to crush him to the ground when he'd realized his favorite son had been planning his doom behind the scenes all along. With Thea's support, Xander had taken down Konstantin and every one of his cronies, cutting the rot from his family and the bank.

Annika's stubbornness was no barrier.

He'd have her and all her secrets before this farce of a marriage was over, and she was out of his life permanently. Maybe then, he could move on from this madness too. A taste of it *had to be* enough.

* * *

Damn it, why had she lost it so spectacularly? What had Xander done except to lay down the law, as was his nature? And worse, why was she taking it personally if he wanted to model her into a dummy Stepford wife when that was what he needed out of their arrangement?

She sat on the luxurious bed and went over what had transpired.

She'd been upset and he'd noticed. And he'd tried to probe. And when she hadn't responded to his demands, he'd needled her. She'd played right into his hands, against her own agenda. She couldn't afford to antagonize him, and it was exactly what she'd done.

After everything she'd planned and executed, bending to Xander's will and transforming herself into some perfect zombie wife was no hardship. God, she'd played so many games and pulled so many cons that she could do it in her sleep. So why was she riling him up when he was the only one who could get her what she needed?

She buried her face in her hands and sighed. She knew exactly why.

She despised it when she was backed into a corner, when she could do nothing but shed tears of rage and powerlessness, and that was how Xander had found her—wounded and hurting and near feral. It had taken him very little to push her over the edge when she'd already been scrambling for a foothold.

It hadn't been easy to say goodbye to the boys, and it hadn't helped to know that she'd be lolling about in luxury for the near future when Killian had admitted—under her forceful questions—that he was close to declaring bankruptcy. He had to sell their house because he couldn't afford mortgage payments.

The very house in which her mother had been happy, the house where her brothers had been born, the house where Annika had hoped to live in the future.

Because of Niven and his damn mind games. He was destroying her stepfather piece by piece because she hadn't toed the line. Because she'd dared find her own bridegroom. Because she was inching closer and closer to getting her hands on her trust fund and to being completely out of his reach.

She needed to wash the day off her and start over. And then she'd apologize to Xander, even if she choked on the words. Somehow, she'd learn to play nice. Five minutes later, she was back to trying to twist herself into unnatural angles to get to the thousand eyelet buttons on the back of her dress.

"I believe that's my duty," Xander said, meeting her gaze in the gleaming chrome of the shower.

"Perks before duties, with me, always," she said, regretting the taunt instantly.

"Let's not forget the reason he gets such an easy rise out of you, my dear Ani," Sebastian had mocked her once. *"You lust after my brother. Always have. Always will."*

Trust that rogue to throw that unpalatable truth in her face.

"If you let me perform my duty first and undress you, the perks will follow. With me, your gratification will not be instant but…long-lasting."

Ani barely managed to hold off her own colorful retort. Turning, she considered him, reaching for the only available strategy. He was right that she couldn't manipulate him. "I agree to all your ridiculous demands."

"Annika—"

"No, let me get this out all at once. The first thing I will do after we land is go hunting for bras. Lock these babies away in a jail," she said, doing a little jiggle of her chest, "even though those horrible underwire thingies bruise my skin like hell. I'll donate my skanky tank tops and ass-baring shorts to charity. I'll cut my cotton boho dresses and make quilts for homeless children. I'll give up drinking and fun and shady exes, and when I feel the urge to steal something, I'll come and tell you so that you can cuff me to your bed. I'll only wear clothes that hide my tats and my belly button ring."

She unraveled the wavy mass of her hair, the bane of her life, and the thick strands fell to her waist. Maybe it was time for a change of image too. It was exhausting to be in a fight against life every single minute of every single day. Maybe she should view this as a short breather in the war she was waging.

"Quite the picture you have painted," Xander said, walking into the room, but leaving the bed in between them. "Shall we address the sudden one-eighty in your attitude?"

Twisting her hair into a knot with a rough tug, she said, "I'll even chop this off and get something sleek and chic and suitable for a rigid banker's perfect, peerless wife."

"No."

"Don't be your perfect wife?"

"Don't cut your hair."

And just like that, it was back in the room again. Electricity hummed in the air, arcing between them, brought in this time by that dark, possessive current in his command.

He hadn't actually praised her hair or said he liked it or

written poems to it as one of her poor fiancés had done, and yet, Annika could feel his desire in her own body like the vibrations from some hidden chip whose button lay in his hands. In his words. In his looks.

"I want a change," she said, her protest weak and late and utterly for principle.

"Are we back to arguing, then?" he said, taking a step around the bed.

Ani ran her palms over opposing shoulders in a bid to cover the fact that the innocent scrape of lace against her breasts had them beading with desire. With each step he took toward her, her skin felt two times too small. And the worst part was that she knew he wouldn't touch her. It was her own desires and demons she was up against.

Taking the bull by the horns, she turned around to present him with her back. Her breaths were shallow as she waited. His fingers landed on the nape of her neck and she jerked, like a fish thrown out of water.

His touch became firm, one hand holding her in place, while he deftly began undoing the buttons. With each inch of skin he bared, Ani felt the rough press of his finger pads leaving a searing trail.

"I want a wedding present," she blurted out. That was it. *Stick to your best role.* She added a bit of complaint to her tone. "Sebastian promised me one."

His fingers moved relentlessly, reaching the middle of her spine. He moved closer, and with one hand on her shoulder blade, he pressed her down. Her hips hit his thighs and instant dampness bloomed between her own.

Ani pressed her hand onto the bed to support her trembling legs, fighting the urge to push back into his solid hard warmth at her back. How was she going to get through this if her panties melted off whenever he touched her?

"And what was my brother getting in return?"

She heard it then—the thick desire in his voice and how he battled it by bringing Sebastian into this place between them where he didn't belong.

"My delightful company."

Now Xander's fingers were at the dip of her spine, and still the buttons continued. "A wedding present? That's supposed to explain your eager agreement?"

"I'm a woman who has her priorities straight and doesn't let anything get in her way, Xander. You'd admire my single-mindedness if you didn't hate me so much."

For the first time since they'd begun the torturous journey down her back, his fingers stilled. His other hand had moved lower too and lay still between her shoulder blades.

Ani clutched the front of her dress as it came away from her skin, releasing flesh it had tortured for hours. "Xander?"

"I do not hate you, Annika."

"Let's not fight about semantics," she said, shaking now that he was working on the last few buttons, right over her buttocks. "I also want an allowance." And because he could feel her trembling body and she hated that it was betraying her like this, she added, "And I'll even let you undress what's underneath—"

"Don't, Ani."

She turned around, that word on his lips searing through her worse than being undressed by him. Tears gathered at the backs of her eyes and she blinked to fight them off. "Don't call me that."

"Why not?"

"Only people I love get to call me that."

His upper lip rolled and Ani braced herself for whatever he would deal. "You'll have one million euros in your bank account within the week—my wedding present. No conditions attached."

Her breath left her in a sudden gush as relief and gratitude flooded her. Maybe Killian could fight to keep the house, continue to send the boys to good schools, even funnel some money back into the business, cover some of those losses Niven had bamboozled him into… "Why a week?"

He laughed then. "Greedy little thing, aren't you? There will be a lot of paperwork to go through before you have a Swiss bank account and it lands in your account. A lot of tax legalities on your end."

"And the big bad banker can't just make all that go away?" she asked, turning.

"Not if I want to maintain my reputation as…" He stilled and stared at her.

The dress fell away, revealing the virginal white silk bustier and a matching thong and garters holding up sheer thigh-highs. Her friend had teased her mercilessly that she finally understood how Ani had tamed the ultimate playboy, Sebastian Skalas.

Ani had simply smiled, hating that she couldn't share the simplest truth with her friend. The veil and the ridiculously lacy dress and the train…they had all been for show, yes.

Her lingerie, though, had been for herself. Desperate to claim something in that farce for herself, she'd gone to town, blowing all the money Thea had given her as a wedding gift on lingerie. Now, she felt a giddy heat and intense gratitude for that crazy decision as Xander's gaze moved over her. Her shoulders and the tops of her breasts, which were indecently pushed up by the bustier, and the strip of her flesh above the low thong…every inch of her skin felt his gaze like a brand.

And that too—that flare of hot want in his eyes, the way he'd stilled, the way his nostrils flared—she'd claim that for herself too. While she wouldn't admit it to him, this hot pulse of wanting between them that gathered momentum like a wildfire was one of the few real things in a life she'd filled with artifice and cunning.

"Come here," Xander said, and she went without question.

He reached out and ran a finger along her collarbone, making her pulse flutter like the wings of a bird desperately making a bid for freedom. "I'll give you an allowance if you agree to one more thing."

Ani nodded, her heart pounding in her chest, hating herself just a little.

He clasped her cheek and tilted her chin up until she had nowhere to go except the stormy, raging gray of his eyes. His words were cold, remote. "You will burn every single piece of clothing you bought for this wedding. For him."

Shock swept through her. He really didn't like that she'd been about to marry Sebastian. Because she wasn't good enough for his brother? Because he himself despised her? Or was there another reason?

"You want me to walk into your home naked?"

"A small detail that will be taken care of in mere minutes." Then his hands were in her hair and his mouth was at her temple and he…nuzzled at her cheek. The movement made her chest rub against his muscled side and that was exquisite torment too, and she just wanted to sink into him, to cling to him, to demand he give her one moment of respite and pleasure after a day of war.

With that grip in her hair, he shuffled her backward with a gentleness that threatened to undo her already fragile grip on her senses. Then his gaze was on her mouth and she licked her lips compulsively, begging him to cover the distance without saying the words.

His mouth quirked. "It is nonnegotiable, Annika. Is that clear?"

She nodded like a chastised child and in the next blink of breath he was walking away, while she grappled with a damp, aching core, heavy breasts, and need rippling through her.

Her legs gave out at the loss of him holding her captive and she flopped onto the bed, as if she were already that puppet and he'd cut her strings. Heart pounding, she wondered what else she'd gotten wrong about this man she'd married. Clearly, he felt a great many things: he was possessive, he was jealous of her relationship with Sebastian, and he'd wanted her long before an accident of fate had brought him to the altar.

Under the hot, pounding shower, Ani realized that despite it all, he'd walked away easily. Effortlessly. Meanwhile, she was reduced to touching her damp, aching folds, her mouth pressed against the gleaming chrome knowing that nothing but his touch would bring relief now.

CHAPTER FIVE

FOR THE TWO days since arriving at the villa in Corfu, all Ani had done was eat, sleep and wander down to the private beach every evening. After showing her to the third story—his private wing that had always been forbidden to her before—Xander had disappeared. The rush of the chopper not a half hour after they'd arrived told her that he'd left for Athens.

Two days of reprieve from not only him but Thea too. Two days of wandering through the house, playing her cello in the huge ballroom with fantastic acoustics on the ground floor, chatting with her brothers on the phone and convincing Killian to accept the money she'd send him soon. He'd only agreed when she'd reminded him how Bug, her middle brother, had flipped out at the idea of having to change schools—a fact she'd learned from Ayaan, her oldest brother.

This morning, knowing that Thea was back, Annika took her time getting dressed. She chose a light blue silk camisole and white linen trousers and a bra from her new wardrobe. Then she braided her still-damp hair, while standing on the terrace that stretched out like an overhang directly into the Ionian Sea.

The magnificent three-story villa had been built right

into the very edge of the first cliff and had multiple terraces, each with gorgeous views. From the first moment she'd visited the villa as a little girl with her mother, the tranquil view of the sea, the beautiful home and the private strip of beach had meant safety and security. Not that she'd known at the time that her mama had been planning to leave her father soon and abandon Annika to him in the process.

Her mother had already been pregnant with Ayaan and Annika's father wouldn't divorce her. As always, Ani wondered for a moment whether her mother had worried that she might lose Ani, or whether her husband would use Ani to punish his wife's infidelity.

The only constant had been her godmother, Thea. Ani's father's interest in her had faded when he'd married Niven's mother following the divorce.

Any hope she'd nurtured of seeing her mama had been dashed, thanks to the bodyguards dogging her every step. But being here with Thea, following Sebastian as he wandered the island, catching flashes of Xander at dinnertime when he'd show her tricks with numbers—the man was a genius when it came to it—had been a balm to her soul. This villa had been a sanctuary to her. A refuge.

Now, standing on the terrace, Ani raised her face to the sky, the April sun kissing her cheeks. But the gorgeous view didn't calm her frantic mind today.

Coming here as Xander's new bride was unsettling in a way she hadn't foreseen. She'd have been in the second story as Sebastian's wife. So why did this feel so… strange? After all these years, it felt like her relationship to the house was morphing. Things were going to change when this farce was over. Was that the reason she felt such dread in her belly?

She and Sebastian had planned to separate a few years down the line; they'd walk away without causing any lasting harm to their friendship, or to her relationship with Thea. The older woman knew very well the odds were stacked against Sebastian sticking it out in matrimony, acknowledging that no one but Ani could even *bring* him to the altar.

But being here as Xander's wife was different. Sharing a private suite with him, having to put on a show for Thea and the world, resisting him and then parting ways...it was going to change everything. Of all the turbulence life had thrown at her, this was the hardest. If she lost Thea and the house...

Suddenly, Ani felt scared and alone and rootless.

When her cell chirped with a text from Thea, who was impatiently holding breakfast for her, Ani wiped the wetness from her cheeks and put her game face on.

Xander kissed his grandmama on her cheek and took the seat opposite her. He'd returned from Athens ten minutes ago, and had been ordered to show for breakfast when all he'd wanted to do was to run up to his suite on the third story and...do what? Pant over his new bride like a randy teenager?

He'd spent two days away, to give them both respite. To get his head screwed on straight. Seeing Annika in lingerie she'd chosen for his twin had made him feel like a caveman. Yes, he wanted her, but this...indefinable possessiveness was neither appropriate nor good.

Pouring himself a cup of dark coffee, he raised a brow at Thea. "No congratulations for me? After you pestered me for months to find a bride?"

"I'm not sure if I should congratulate you or disown you

for your actions," she said, coming straight to the point as always. "She was Sebastian's intended. God knows no other woman can straighten Sebastian. They have friendship and understanding and similarities that were a good foundation for marriage. And you…" her mouth pursed with disapproval, bordering on distaste "…swooped in and stole her. I taught you better than this. I taught you to watch out for him."

Xander hated disappointing his grandmother, the one responsible adult he'd ever known. But for the first time, he felt extreme resentment toward her. He rubbed a hand over his face. "You have a sharp enough mind not to forget that your favorite grandson went missing minutes before the wedding. He *left* her there."

She harrumphed. "You couldn't stand as a placeholder? Pretend to be him and give her back when he returned?"

"And you couldn't, for once in my life, not ask me to consider Sebastian's needs or this family's needs or the great Skalas name before my own? You couldn't for once think of my wishes, Grandmama?"

A stunned look came into her eyes. "Alexandros—"

"It is done. She is my wife," he said, cutting her off. It continued to be disconcerting how easily he was ruffled when his new wife was the topic. "I'll not explain myself to anyone, not even you."

"Fine. I will put my concerns for Sebastian aside. You… have been voluble in the past about how you can't stand Ani—that she's here every summer, that I am fond of her, that she… You barely tolerate her presence in our lives, Alexandros. What am I to think of this development? How do I know you will not shred that child to pieces with your impossible demands and controlling nature? You are not an easy man to live with."

Xander laughed, the sound full of scornful self-deprecation. "So I am to be molded into a controlling monster to save your family and its fortunes and then be castigated for the very same?"

Thea blanched and her stiff mouth wobbled. She suddenly looked very much like the seventy-eight-year-old woman that they forgot she was, for her will was made of steel. A tired sigh escaped her. "She has fought far too many battles in her short life."

"While I do not know what they are," he said, curiosity gouging a hole through him, "I can reassure you that it has made her fierce enough to take me on."

Thea blinked, opened her mouth and then closed it. "So you do see her," she said with almost savage satisfaction. Then she frowned anew. "Unless you've used her desperation to your own advantage and roped her into—"

"Isn't it interesting that I have more faith in her than you do," Xander interrupted, "for all that you claim to love her?"

"She does not know you like I do."

"On the contrary," Xander said, the words full of a recently discovered conviction. "Annika knows exactly who I am. I will even admit that I have fallen for her act…like every other man out there."

Before Thea could interrogate him more, Annika appeared over the slope, one of those twinkling smiles from her repertoire stitched onto her lips. But Xander saw the vacuous nature of it now. He leaned back in his seat, watching her. Two days spent away from her hadn't dimmed his awareness of her one bit.

In a simple silk camisole and linen pants that flaunted her long legs, she looked every inch the sleek, sophisticated woman he'd demanded she mold herself into. Her makeup, if she wore any, was light. With the dark circles under her eyes gone, she looked rested, even poised, as if she'd simply removed the reckless, flighty party girl filter and put on the perfectly groomed, boring socialite filter. Like they were all just masks for her and the real woman was buried deep beneath. Or even lost, he thought with a vague sense of discontent.

As she came closer, he noted the diamond circle pendant on a gold chain at her neck and the platinum Rolex on her wrist and diamond studs at her ears—every piece chosen by him. For a man who'd never personally bought a gift—his ex-fiancée and current business partner, Diana, was too practical to even expect that he would—he'd enjoyed walking into a jewelry boutique and selecting pieces for Annika.

When she tucked one stray wild lock of hair behind her ear, he saw the last piece on her finger. Different from the rest, it was a large bloodred ruby set in a gold ring—an antique Indian piece from a specialized collection, he'd been informed, that had once belonged to a warrior princess.

He'd bought it on impulse—though it didn't match the dull, almost boring, elegance of the rest of the collection—because it had reminded him of her, of who he was beginning to see she was beneath all the armor she covered herself in. And against all his own rules, he had wanted her to have one thing she'd appreciate.

Shooting to his feet, he gave in to the insane idea of messing up the boring veneer he'd insisted on. "Excuse me, Grandmama, but I'd like to kiss my wife," he announced to a shocked Thea.

My wife...

He liked the sound of that very much.

Annika stumbled on the downward slope, even though she was wearing flat sandals, when she saw Xander prowling toward her, as if he'd set his prey in his sights. He moved like a predator too, all casual grace and economic gait. But instead of being scared, she felt a pulse of excitement, remembering his hands on her back.

In the next blink he was there, catching her with an arm around her waist. Her chest banged into his, knocking the breath out of her. She'd barely taken hold of her senses as she drowned in the rich, ocean scent of him when he pulled her closer.

Palm at the base of her neck, fingers spread upward into her hair, he tilted her face to meet his. The tips of their noses touched, and his exhales teased her lips. "Xander, what—"

"*Kalimera*, Kyria Skalas."

It took her a while to remember how words were made. When she did, they came out all husky. "Good morning, Kyrios Skalas."

"Two days away from each other, *ne*?" he teased, though the amusement didn't reach his gray eyes. "Let's make it look like they have been unbearable."

It was all the warning she received before his mouth found hers.

Ani moaned, the idea of protest not even a passing thought. Tendrils of pleasure shot through her and she grabbed onto him, sending her fingers on a quest. He smelled like dark decadence, like all the sinful desires she'd never let weaken her. Like the deepest, darkest longing she'd hidden away, even from herself.

If he'd punished her again, if he'd tried to assert his dominance over her like he'd done at the wedding, she could have mounted some kind of resistance. She would have. But the cunning, ruthless bastard that he was, he switched strategy.

This kiss was nothing like the last one. This was…a tender exploration, a gentle teasing, an invitation to play. As if they were equals and there were no rules except pleasure and no destination to reach. As if there was no muddled past or murky future, nothing but the heady present.

And she played. Shamelessly. Selfishly. Opening her mouth for him to sweep into. Tangling her tongue with his. Sucking at the tip of his. Rubbing herself against his chest with an urgency she was beginning to understand only now. She was already addicted to him—his brand of possessiveness, his dares, his mouth. And she knew why. He made her forget her life, her troubles, her self-control, her principles. He made her want to be swept away instead of constantly, relentlessly swimming upstream.

"Xander," she whispered, needing more.

His palms drifted down her back and the pressure of his lips increased in direct proportion to her unspoken demand.

Ani found herself losing her foothold on rationality and reality as the gentle play broke new ground. With hungry nips and eager pants and shallow breaths, she followed him as he funneled more and more pleasure into her until she was pressing herself against him with wanton abandon. She raked her fingernails over the nape of his neck when he stopped and dug her teeth into the pad of his lower lip.

A rough grunt shuddered out of him, his hips jerking

against hers, and the shocking press of his arousal made her knees tremble. She felt like she was deep under water, weighed down by sensation, floating along on pure pleasure, without a care.

Hands clasped her cheeks tenderly and she opened her eyes.

Xander looked as ravaged as she felt within. His designer haircut was all mussed and on his lower lip there was an indentation of her teeth.

Ani jerked back, remembering what she'd done. "I'm sorry. I..."

He touched his finger to the mark she'd left on his lip, something hot and slick coming awake in his gray eyes. "Everything is a lie with us, *ne*? You don't have to apologize for what is not."

She nodded, licking her swollen, sensitive lips and felt the pang somewhere else.

"Especially when we both like it," he said, somehow the words full of both tenderness and raw claiming. "That should go some way toward pacifying Thea," he said.

Ani looked up, heart in her throat. Uncoiling herself from around him, she glanced at Thea, who was watching them without blinking. That shrewd gaze brought her back to reality with a thump. Embarrassment welled up within her—she'd almost climbed him as if he were a tree!—and she tried to step away from him.

Xander's hold tightened. "There's nothing to be ashamed about either."

Ani sighed, knowing it was too late anyway. "Is she angry?"

"With me, yes. Not you," he said, straightening her rumpled blouse with a casual possessiveness she'd never, not in ten lifetimes, expected of him. He took her right hand in his and brought her knuckles to his mouth. "All you need to do is play into the narrative that I'm the big bad wolf that has gobbled you up. Gullible and guileless, upset by Sebastian's abandonment, you were broken up about your future when I swooped in heroically and saved you. Maybe you've been secretly in love with me for years, were distraught you couldn't have me, which is why you settled for second best and—"

"That makes me sound like an awful human being," Ani said, pushing at his chest and stumbling. She didn't know whether to laugh or cry at the tale he was spinning.

He caught her and she saw the unspoken question in his eyes. The lies in which she'd draped herself were too horrible to let stand. "Xander, about Sebastian and me—"

"Leave it, Annika."

Their gazes held, battling it out, neither willing to give an inch. Until she did, shaking, despite the balmy weather. "Love is too big a lie, especially when it's about you and me. And Thea has never thought me guileless."

"No. And yet, she's so protective of you, *ne*? Grandmama does not suffer—"

"Empty-headed twits like me?" she said, feeding him back his own words.

His expressive mouth flattened. "I'm not the first man to fall for your wiles."

Heart thudding, she scoffed. "You make me sound like a veritable femme fatale."

"Thea not only loves you but respects you," he said, ignoring her jab. "I did not see the distinction until now."

Suddenly, Ani felt like one of those bugs her second brother collected. He never hurt them, he didn't torment them, but he studied them constantly, fascinated. Now she had caught Xander's...interest. Frenzied excitement bubbled over in every cell at that adolescent dream taking shape. This was *so* not her plan!

Tucking her into his side, he shuffled her toward Thea, instantly shifting his stride to match hers. "The one thing you need to convince her of is your commitment to me."

"You said she's angry with you. Why?"

"She thinks I stole you out from under my poor, naive twin's nose."

"Wait," Ani said, forcing him to stop. A strand of her hair got caught in his jacket button, gleaming golden brown against the black fabric. She tugged at it, working through the knot in her head. Looking up, she caught his surprise at how easily she touched him and flushed. "That's not right or fair."

"What?"

"I might not like you or agree with you on most things, but I'll not support this ridiculous theory that you took advantage of me or conned Sebastian—*as if* he can be conned. Does she know him at all?"

Xander shrugged.

"She's always had a soft spot for Sebastian. It makes her blind to his true nature," Ani continued. "And she can't now complain about your ruthlessness and demand for perfection and your brilliant strategic mind when she has employed them to great benefit to protect the Skalas name and legacy."

His shock was a palpable twang in the air around them. He looked away, jaw so tight that she wondered if she'd crossed some invisible line between them. When he turned back to her, his gray eyes gleamed with a dark humor. "Not only a wife who'll follow my every rule but a champion too, Annika?" He ran the tip of his finger over her jaw. "Careful, *matia mou*. I might never give you up."

Ani shivered at the silky claim.

"Right now, you're angry with Sebastian, so your loyalties have shifted," he said, rejecting her impassioned speech in one moment.

For once, his accusation that she was flighty didn't bother her because there was a greater truth she couldn't unsee. Sebastian, for all he'd agreed to help her, was slippery, his motivations a labyrinthine haze that no one could really pierce. Not even his twin. He'd been a good friend to her, to the best of his ability, but Xander...was the opposite.

Once he gave his word, he'd move heaven and earth to keep it. Ruthless as he was, he also claimed intense loyalty in his staff, for he looked after them, donated generously to their children's education and retirement funds and was renowned for his fair and equitable practices in the banking world.

The sudden intimacy of their conversation, the idea of her and Xander together against the world, made warmth blossom in her chest. As if she now had an army at her beck and call. As if she wasn't alone in her fight against Niven anymore.

"I know marrying me suited your needs too," she said, making sure she met his gray gaze. "And you drive a hard bargain. But you didn't have to step in as you did. For that I'm grateful."

Hands tucked into his pockets, he watched her, unblinking and radiating intense dislike. "There's no kindness behind my actions."

"Yes, well, being weighed down in diamonds can go a

long way toward making a girl grateful," she said, reaching for that easy flippancy, refusing to give up her conviction that his actions meant more than just a mutually convenient transaction, in a life where there had been very few.

"Why did you propose to Sebastian if you have feelings for Alexandros?" Thea demanded the moment Ani sat down.

Luckily or not, Xander's phone had rung right when they'd had reached Thea and he'd excused himself. Annika took a bite of a buttery croissant, prolonging the moment. "You're the one who suggested I should propose to Sebastian," she said, her hand shaking as she poured herself some thick, dark coffee.

This was what she'd dreaded: lying to the one person who'd always stood by her.

Thea clamped her wrist in a hard grip, forcing Ani to meet her eyes. "I will forgive you for anything...except playing my grandsons against each other."

Hurt sliced through Ani. "You know me better than that."

"I thought so too. But that kiss looked very real. Why agree to my idea then?" Her gaze was a laser burn on Ani's skin. "Unless you and Xander have made a dangerous deal."

Annika went for as much truth as she could, seeing Thea was dangerously close to it. "Look, Sebastian disappeared at the last minute, despite knowing how much was at stake for me. He left Xander to do his dirty work. Xander...tried to console me and something happened. Something the both of us have ignored for a...long time. It led to...more." When Thea's stare remained unrelenting, Ani let some of her own confusion and tiredness infuse her words. "I'm tired, Thea. Tired of fighting Niven. Tired of seeing my stepfather and my brothers suffer because of me, of…being unrelentingly strong. So, yes, when things went too far with Xander, I told him everything and he offered to marry me. Of course I jumped on the chance. I want a protector, a provider, and even you'll agree, Xander is the best choice. I'll do my best to be the wife he wants."

Thea's anger melted like the last remnant of snow under a suddenly dazzling spring sun. She took Ani's hand in hers, her eyes full of the same affection and compassion that had always nurtured her. "I can see the passion between you two but you're both—"

"We're both willing to do whatever it takes. In that, we're very similar."

Looking thoughtful, her godmother nodded.

"Maybe you think I'm not good enough for the Skalas heir, eh?"

Thea smiled. "Or perhaps you could be the one who brings my stubborn, arrogant grandson to his knees?"

"I can only dream." Ani laughed, knowing she could never. She didn't even want to. Or so she kept telling herself.

Reaching out, Thea palmed Ani's cheek. "But what about you, Ani?"

"You're the one who taught me that practicality is more important than—"

"What about love and freedom and your music and all the dreams you've held on to for so long? What about your longing for a family and children and a big house and a man who adores you? What about not letting your mother's mistakes dictate your own—"

Annika's neck prickled and she felt Xander behind her, like a phantom pulse inside her body. The last thing she wanted was for him to know anything about her real hopes and dreams. He didn't have a right to them.

Tilting her chin up in a playful gesture, she met his gaze upside down.

Questions swirled in his gray eyes, his mouth a taut line of displeasure. Reaching for his jaw, she ran the ruby from her ring against his chin. "This piece…" she said, heart in her throat, "it's different from the rest of the collection. So…unique. I've never seen anything like it. Does it have a history? Where did you find it?"

"Magdalena found it," he said, throwing out his assistant's name with a careless casualness.

Under the guise of holding her hand up and studying it, Ani beat back the prick of hurt. Just because Xander was on her side didn't mean he'd suddenly buy her meaningful gifts.

"That charity gala at Lake Geneva in two weeks' time?" he said to Thea. "Annika and I will attend."

Thea's gaze swept over where his fingers lingered on Annika's shoulder. "It will be the first time in sixteen years that a Skalas will attend. The media attention will be too much for her, Alexandros."

"Is it significant if we attend?" Annika asked.

Grandmother and grandson stared at each other before Xander said, "My father did a lot of damage to our reputation and our business the last time he attended the gala. He lost clients' trust and their hard-earned money. Grandmama has done her best to repair some of it."

Using Xander's genius brain, no doubt. "Why haven't you gone all these years?"

"Only the chairman of the Skalas Bank is invited and

while Thea has been managing it as a proxy, there hasn't been one in a while."

"So if you go now, it's like an informal declaration to the world that you'll be the next chairman, *ne*?" Annika pressed the issue shamelessly, wanting to get it over with, both this discussion and the inevitable prize Xander wanted.

Thea shot them both a hard look.

Shaking inside, she clamped her hands over Xander's arms around her neck. "What?" she said, keeping her tone casual and throwing a charming laugh at the end of it. "You've dangled the position in front of Xander for years now, making it conditional. We all know it should be his already."

"I have a fierce champion now, Thea," Xander said, his voice silky smooth and full of suppressed laughter.

Thea bared her teeth in a smile. "I begin to see what you mean when you say you two are very similar." Then she sighed and addressed Xander. "Let me throw you both a reception here first. She can attend next year."

Leaning down, he rubbed his cheek against Ani's, making her shudder from head to toe. "I have waited for this moment for a long time. If you wish to lend her support, you can accompany us. If not, help Ani with her wardrobe and the politics. I have that delegation from Japan to deal with this week."

"What about a honeymoon, Alexandros?" Thea asked, challenge in every regal line of her face. "What about giving your young bride a little of your time before you toss her into a sea of sharks?"

His long fingers cupped Annika's chin from behind and he pressed a soft kiss to her temple. Her senses reeled from all the possessive little touches. For a man who locked away desires and wants and emotions with an inhuman, steely ruthlessness, Xander sure touched her a lot.

"All the years of training you have unknowingly given her have made her perfect for me, Grandmama. Annika does not dwell in silly dreams and naive hopes. And what better way to adjust to each other than this trip?"

So he'd heard Thea's mention of her silly dreams.

His words haunted Annika for the rest of the week as she prepared to present herself to the world as Alexandros Skalas's prized young wife for the first time.

CHAPTER SIX

ANI RAN UP the stairs to the third story, without slowing her pace. Her thigh muscles groaned and her chest felt as if it was gasping for air but she kept going until she reached the vast bedroom with an open layout and a view of the sea on one side.

In the three weeks since they'd arrived at the villa, the constants in her day were running and endless shopping while being tutored in the utterly boring world of finance politics by Thea. Which made for an easy, slow life. But with her mind on how Killian was making out and the utter quiet from Niven since the wedding, plus all the forced intimacy with Xander and her in the same bedroom, tiring herself out by running up and down the cliff and the entire perimeter of the private stretch of beach was the only thing keeping Ani sane.

With Thea watching them like a hawk, it was all Ani could do to spend time on the third story, whose every inch smelled like Xander. Thank goodness the man worked a bazillion hours, mostly out of his Athens headquarters.

Her thighs and quads quaked as she chugged water from her bottle, pouring some over her head. With Xander gone, she'd been able to play her cello to her heart's content.

Kicking her shoes off, Ani tore off the packaging from a

new bodywash that Thea had bought her and took a whiff of it. Then she pulled off her sweaty T-shirt, lost her shorts and entered the bathroom in her neon-pink sports bra and matching panties to find Xander stepping out of the shower with a thick white towel around his hips.

Ani stilled, clutching the bottle of bodywash to her chest. But the damage was done because she'd already taken in the taut stretch of olive skin with just the right amount of chest hair; defined pecs and a washboard stomach, with a trail of dark hair disappearing into the towel...

A soft, loose heat lashed through her, making her aware of every inch of her own skin. Hair slicked back with wetness, and water drops clinging to his olive skin, he was the exact teenage fantasy she'd indulged in. Only, he was solid and real this time *and* she had a right to look and touch and do more, if she wanted.

He'd made it more than clear that he was all for working this out of their systems; probably even assumed that it was an easy decision for her. As easy as proposing marriage to Sebastian one day and jumping into bed with him the next. It was exactly the image she'd nurtured. She'd made herself into a number of unsavory things, to make sure the men Niven picked for her would reject her. Nothing in her life had ever been fully her choice.

Unlike her, however, Xander didn't stop and stare. He didn't even blink. It was as if Annika standing there, gaping at him, was no big deal. As if he was used to women strolling through his private bathroom every day.

He wasn't, Ani knew for a fact. For one thing, Thea would not allow either brother to bring their *partners* to this home, which was only for Skalas wives.

For another, Xander—unlike Ani and Sebastian—was

extra-extra-protective of his private life. She knew only of one attachment he'd had in all these years and that was only because that woman had been in Xander's life forever as a childhood friend, college mate and business partner, all rolled into one. He'd been engaged to Diana Van Duerson for three years.

Hadn't she spent all three of those summers living in the utmost fear that she'd come across this perfect, mythical woman who met Xander's standards—or worse, see him kiss her or hold her or...something. She'd been a very angsty sixteen-year-old.

Why had the engagement ended? Was that why not one woman that Thea had paraded in front of him had caught his interest?

The thought of him still being in love with Ms. Van Duerson made bile rise up in Ani's throat. Or was that the green smoothie she'd forcibly chugged before the run?

Moving to one of the dual vanity sinks, Xander whipped out his shaving brush and lathered his cheeks and chin with an efficiency he seemed to employ universally in life. "Good run?"

She panted out a *yes*, words refusing to rise to her lips.

"Are you packed?" he asked, meeting her eyes in the large mirror.

"What?" Ani said, stepping further in, captivated by the muscled planes of his back and the divot right above his—

"For what?"

"We fly early tomorrow morning to Geneva."

"Almost."

"The shower is all yours," he said, grabbing a razor.

"That's fine. I'm..."

Covered as his mouth was in shaving cream, Ani couldn't be sure but she thought his mouthed twitched. "I won't peek, Annika. Unless you want me to."

"Stop playing with me, Xander."

"I like playing with you," he said, though there was nothing playful about his tone. Like everything about him, this too was straightforward and ruthless in a way she couldn't hide from. He swiped the razor with practiced ease over his jaw and even that was a thing to watch. "It's the only time I know I'm dealing with the real you."

The bottle of bodywash fell from her hands and Ani's breath turned to shallow pants.

And then he looked at her. And looked. And looked. His gaze lingered nowhere in particular and yet she felt it like a phantom touch on her breasts, her belly and even lower, where she wanted his eyes and fingers and mouth and… more. Desire lapped through her in lazy waves, making her nipples bead behind the thin Lycra of her sports bra and he noticed that too.

Ani clenched her thighs and then flushed bright red. Because he saw that too. He also let her see that her body pleased him, covered as it was in sweat and dust and sand from the beach. Somehow, it wasn't intrusive or invasive. And she knew then that he'd liked her eyes on his body too, that he'd found pleasure in the fact that it aroused her. And it was such a Xander thing too—not letting any emotions or hesitation pollute this.

"I don't know what to say to that. How to fight this," she said, baring her confusion.

He frowned and continued shaving. "You're aware of the draw you hold for men."

She scoffed, feeling as if there were a million sensors set into her skin, every single one of them lighting up anytime he was near. "The draw has always been my fortune. And anyway, you're not most men."

"Is that a good thing or a bad thing?"

"It's a thing," she blurted out, unable to dissemble.

His gaze held hers. A world of questions and answers lobbied back and forth between them. Pulling her gaze away with effort, she bent to pick up the bottle and groaned at a sudden shooting pain at the back of her thigh.

Instantly Xander was shuffling her to the lip of the monstrous bathtub, his hand on her bare hip. Once he was sure she was balanced on the edge, he pulled her leg up with an infinite tenderness that made her shiver. When was the last time anyone had tended to her? Or watched over her with such…gentleness?

Never.

He cursed when he saw the fist-sized muscle bruise on the back of her thigh. "You shouldn't run on this."

"I'll go mad if I don't," she replied, trying to get to her feet.

"Sit down, Annika," he bit out in that low voice, like he used to when he caught her in the middle of some prank Sebastian had instigated.

He returned, clad in loose sweatpants, with a spray and a cold compress. When he gently pressed his fingers around the bruise, she couldn't swallow her grimace. On his knees, he bent closer, his warm breath caressing her skin. "You'll damage the tendon permanently if you don't take care of this."

Ani had the most overwhelming urge to run her hands

through his thick hair, to lean forward and press her mouth to his shoulder, to sink into his capable hands.

"How will you run away from me then? And from yourself?"

"You're taking the whole 'protect and cherish' part of our vows too far. There's no one here to watch us."

He leaned back on his haunches, his hand still cupping her knees. "You seem to have forgotten all the scrapes Sebastian got you into which I got you out of, every summer you visited."

Ani smiled, remembering the glorious sun-kissed days when she'd loved to follow Sebastian about, when she'd lived to get a rise out of Xander. "Sebastian set you up every time and still you came. I think, deep down—" she poked a finger at his granite-hard chest "—you loved playing the hero."

She snatched her hand back as the gray of his eyes deepened. She frowned. "Why did you, Xander? You must have known that Sebastian wouldn't have let me get hurt."

"Like the time he left you napping in the branches of an eight-foot tree when you were thirteen? You'd have broken every bone in your body if you'd fallen," he said, shooting to his feet, every inch of him taut with remembered tension.

Ani was stuck in that moment in the past, though, submerged in the hazy sunshine, the strawberries she'd glutted herself on, the thick, pungent smell of roses surrounding her as she'd suddenly startled awake at Xander's gritted calling of her name. "You'd just returned from that big board meeting where you took your father on. In a white shirt with the cuffs rolled back, tie barely loosened, and you came running to that orange grove…and called my name." Even back then, Xander had worked tirelessly against his father to save the bank, while Sebastian had lazed his days away.

"My charming twin doesn't know his limits. Whether it's stupid stunts or pushing our father—" He bit off the rest, turning away from her with a sudden edge to his movements.

Ani stared at his muscled back and the tense shoulders, his body a map to his emotions. It shocked her, this unveiling of what lay beneath his control, his discipline, his ruthlessness. That day too, it had been fear beneath his vibrating anger.

Xander had always possessed an overdeveloped sense of responsibility toward the people in his sphere—something Thea shamelessly exploited to push her own agenda when he was young.

He'd punched Sebastian in the mouth that day, all while cradling Ani against his chest, as if she were precious. Sebastian had grinned through a bloody mouth, as if he was the victor in a game for which only he knew the rules. Xander hated violence in any form and yet, he'd lost control that day. Over her. He'd been worried about her, enough to come running, enough to get into a fight with his twin.

Ani grabbed the edge of the marble tub, not knowing what to do with the realization that Xander had cared about her once upon a time. Until suddenly, he didn't. The loathing of the last few years had been so vehement that it had distorted all the good times.

What had changed? Was it simply her party girl persona that had put him off? Her supposed greed that disgusted his lofty morals? Would he tell her if she asked? Did she want to know?

"Sebastian liked—still likes—provoking you. You must know that."

Xander splashed water onto his face. And then he was in front of her, looking down at her, disdain dripping from each word, flipping the energy in the room to that pulsing contempt. "After the whole wedding fiasco, you still trust Sebastian, but not me?"

Ani wished she could tell him how much she wanted to give herself over to his capable hands, as she'd told Thea. How much she wanted to give in to this…heat between them. She licked her lower lip, suddenly sick of all the lies swirling between them.

You pushed me away, rejected me, looked at me with contempt in your eyes.

She locked the baffled hurt away, as she'd done before too. "I can't."

A bitter twist to his mouth, he was almost out the bathroom when he stopped. "I ran into your stepbrother the other day."

"What? Where?"

"At a charity auction in NYC last week."

Her throat felt like hot coals had been raked through it. "What…what did he say?"

"He walked up to me, introduced himself, and said congratulations. Invited us to his Hamptons estate. Insisted I tell you that he's sad you had the wedding when he was out of town, that you shouldn't spend a minute worrying about Killian or your brothers because he'll make sure they're all okay."

Ani shot to her feet, feeling urgency creep up under her skin. Niven was turning the screws tighter and tighter.

"Annika?" Xander said, turning around.

She shoved past him, her thoughts in a whirl. She wanted so much to tell Xander about the implied threat in the message Niven had conveyed through him, how the mention of Niven triggered a rage and helplessness in her. But she'd fought her battles alone for so long and that memory about Xander holding her to his chest only told her how foolish it was to put her faith in him.

Xander recognized the look in Annika's eyes before she ran. He'd seen the very same in Sebastian's eyes and his own when he'd looked in the mirror a long time ago, before he'd learned that the trick to defeat his father was to not show it.

It was fear.

Seeing Annika's expressive face turn colorless made him want to pound something into a pulp. He stared at himself in the mirror, shocked at the overwhelming intensity of it. He had no prior experience with these swings in emotion, loathed being under the grip of such intense desires as she provoked in him. His expectation that he'd defeat this obsession with her once he had her in his life seemed impossible now.

With each passing day and night, he was more invested in the puzzle that was Annika. The question Thea had asked her when she'd thought him out of earshot had disturbed him enough that he had fled to Athens to drown himself in work.

What about love and family and all your other dreams?

Being a very logical person, he looked for reasons as to why it bothered him so much. Maybe because he'd thought her one thing and, as always, Annika kept turning all his assumptions upside down. Maybe because he'd always been extremely competitive and a stubborn part of him wanted to give her everything she wanted.

He could simply ask Thea about her, but he didn't want to betray his confusion to her hawklike attention. And more importantly, he wanted to hear it all from Annika's mouth. He wanted her to give him her confidences and secrets and fears willingly. He had an inexplicable need to have her come to him, to have her depend on him, to have her... need him.

And he would, too. He would unravel every secret, every fear, until she was bare to him. Then maybe he could kick this as he would any other addiction.

He found her in the expansive closet, pulling and discarding shirts and dresses with a near frenzy. Drawers with expensive lingerie lay open, silky wisps of lace overflowing out of them. Whatever she was looking for was probably lost in the mess.

One side of the closet was intact—his suits and ties and shirts and leather shoes and loafers all kept in their designated place by staff who knew how obsessively particular he was with his things.

The other side of it was a wreckage with Annika at the center of it. Unaware of his arrival, she tugged her sports bra off over her head, giving him glimpses of silky smooth brown skin. Then she grabbed an old T-shirt—his university T-shirt, to be exact—and pulled it on. Something feral sparked inside him as he saw a pile of them had been transferred from his side to hers.

Tall as she was, the T-shirt barely covered her upper thighs. With a rough growl, she pulled free her braid that was stuck in the neckline. Sneaking her hands under its hem, she pulled her panties down. The glimpse of a shapely buttock held him in thrall.

It was like offering a starving man a glimpse of delicious morsels he could only see but not consume. But even more than the arousal flooding through him was the tenderness she provoked. She looked like a wounded animal and he desperately wanted to soothe her. And the only way to do that, it seemed, was to rile her.

"You said you'd finished packing," he said, unable to look away from the chaos she created wherever she went.

She turned around and blinked. "Divorce me for being a last-minute packer."

"Forget packing, this is a...disaster zone! Like the bridal suite. Do you always ransack through your stuff like some deranged raccoon?"

Her mouth twitched, that wicked gleam returning to her eyes. "Wait till you see what I've done to the study."

"My study is a no-go area for anyone," he said, unable to keep the horror out of his voice.

"Not to your wife. Isn't married life fun?" Grabbing a drawer full of makeup, she emptied it out in front of the large, full-length mirror. Tubes of lipstick and eyeliners and mascara rolled around. She pushed the heap to the ground, emptied another bag and started over. Then it was a tiny bag of coins. Then a bag of rocks—actual rocks, still covered in dirt and moss and—

The nerve in his temple started thrumming. "If this is the game you want to play, you should know I will win it."

Smacking her lips, she beckoned him with a finger. The audacity of the gesture made him want to kiss the hell out of her. Or pound it out of her in the best way he knew.

"You know what, Xander? Let's make a bet."

"Sebastian has ruined you."

"And yet, I have the most fun when I play with you," she said, holding his gaze.

"What is the bet?"

"If you can walk through this mess and come to me, I'll pack right now, while you stand there, to your satisfaction. I'll even let you...kiss me again. Just for the fun of it. No audience."

Xander saw the pattern then—the more cornered Annika felt, the harder she came out swinging recklessly at the world. So many of her scandalous actions could be neatly slotted into place then. "That's a dangerous bluff, *pethi mou*. It might mean that our first time together is on that hard marble bench in the middle of a very messy closet when I'd prefer taking my time on a comfortable bed."

She cleared her throat, even as her gaze drew a tantalizing trail down his bare chest. "That's very...cocky of you."

He raised one shoulder even as he considered a strategic route to get to her through the mess. His right eye twitched at the idea. "You and I both know we won't be able to stop with a kiss one of these days. I have simply accepted the inevitability of it."

A blush ran up her sharp cheekbones. "More steps and fewer words, Xander."

The very thought of entering the center of it made his muscles clench up tight. Even as he fought the trigger, his body—like Pavlov's dog—remembered the punishment such a mess had earned him once.

Shame burned him at his inability to shred the memory, his inability to fight the conditioned response even as a thirty-four-year-old man. He thrived on keeping his cool and control in the most challenging situations at work and in life but this…this threw him.

Whatever Annika saw in his face—and Xander loathed the very thought that she might be privy to his internal fight—she lowered that belligerent chin. "You know what? This is silly. I'll just finish packing."

Without waiting, she marched back around the labyrinthine closet and tried to pull an overnight bag from the top shelf. Reaching her, Xander pulled it down. When she turned around, he raised a brow.

"It was a stupid bet."

"Which I won," he said like a petulant teenager.

She smiled then and it was a soft, sweet one that she used to give him as a kid. The ones that used to feel like a balm to his soul. The ones he'd gotten so addicted to that he—

"I'll make sure I don't create such a mess, moving forward."

His heart gave a thump. It was a very strange feeling that she invoked—her sudden ferocious claims where she championed him, or supported him or, like now, sought somehow to protect him from hurt.

No one had ever done that for him, not even Thea. And it stuck to his skin like something unwanted and sticky and painful. He didn't know how to sit with it. He didn't want it. And the only response he'd taught himself for those occasions—a blistering set-down—rose to his lips but he couldn't release it. There was an earnest sweetness to how she'd made that offer.

"You can create all the mess you want here," he said, putting on an air of condescension that she hated. "No one else will be privy to our personal life, *ne*? Especially since it pushes you to offer me sweet, tantalizing deals in return for my…hardship."

A surprised smile broke through. "A kiss, then?"

"A secret."

"Way to bring down a girl's confidence," she said, looking adorably put out. "What secret?"

"Tell me why you're scared of your stepbrother."

"I'm not," she said automatically. "He's just a…greedy asshole who wants to steal my trust fund." When he simply stared at her, she said, "Even with Papa gone, he continues this twisted legacy of controlling me. You understand not letting someone like that win, don't you?"

"I also understand the confusion left behind by a mother who didn't choose me over her own happiness or her freedom. As does Sebastian, *ne*?"

Ani fell back against the wall.

Konstantin Skalas's cruelty to his sons was not news to her. He had wielded different weapons over them, demanding perfection and ruthlessness and order, and meting out punishment for the smallest flaws.

While Xander had striven for and won his father's approval, Konstantin's treatment of the chaotic, artistic Sebastian had been intolerable. While the brothers had never let Konstantin break them by turning them against each other, he had left invisible scars all the same. And their mother had simply fled, leaving the twins to the mercy of a man she couldn't live with. "You never mention her," she whispered, her mind reeling.

Xander shrugged. "She left. There was nothing to do but make my peace with it. Sebastian is the one who still hopes to find her."

Suddenly, so much about Sebastian made sense. "I understand his hope."

"Do you?" Xander said with a bite. "It is a foolish pursuit to chase someone who does not want to be found. To want someone who does not want you. It is a madness that has consumed him for years."

"And you? Is it easy to write her off, Xander? To forget her? To move forward as if she hadn't been a part of your life once?" Ani didn't know why she was poking at a wound that had to hurt and yet she wanted something from him. An admission that he missed a woman who'd left him two decades ago? A glimpse of his pain? A fracture in his control? When had she turned so bloodthirsty?

"I didn't have the luxury to dwell on what life would have been if she hadn't left. I chose to deal with the monster she left us with, to protect Sebastian from him, to repair the damage he did to the bank, to its staff, to the clients who trusted him. There was no one else to do it. Konstantin left Thea a wreck."

She had known he'd stepped up to help Thea, that he'd once taken a beating meant for Sebastian, that he'd driven Konstantin out of the company, that with the trust of two good men in the company, he'd made millions at the age of twenty-one.

And yet now, after all these years, after all the prejudices and hurt she'd held on to like a shield, she saw Xander with the understanding of a woman who had fought her own monsters. In the process, they had both acquired battle scars. And who was she to say hers were more justified than his?

She felt the most insane urge to throw her arms around him, to hold him, to just be with him in this moment when they could see each other without masks and veils, in all their unbroken glory. But to do so would be to let her guard down, not just in front of him, but for herself.

"Why did you mention her, Xander?" she asked, curious.

He rested one long finger against her temple, while his thumb softly patted her cheek. The tenderness in the gesture floored her. "If you're fighting this battle for yourself, do it. But do not carry out some misunderstood revenge on your mother's behalf. Do not try to champion someone who should have championed you. Do not imagine a different past because all it will do is ruin your future."

"I've already ruined it," she said with a sudden laugh that barely covered her tears. She'd called him emotionally ruthless and yet he had seen into the heart of her so easily.

Yes, she didn't want Niven to win. But a part of her wanted to earn her mother's approval from beyond the grave by saving the sons she had loved. By proving that she was worthy of a love that should have been her right anyway. "By tying myself to you."

He smiled. "One day, I will hear you admit that I saved you, Annika Skalas."

CHAPTER SEVEN

ANNIKA HAD BEEN pretending to be a vacuous airhead for hours, playing into the narrative Xander's ex, Diana Van Duerson, eagerly spun by talking about banking and finance in a way that no layperson could understand. In between the hundred questions she asked Xander at their dinner table, she kept saying "Oh, I'm sorry, this must be over your head," to Ani, followed by a patronizing pat on her arm.

It was their second evening at the charity gala, and Ani was beginning to wonder if this was why Xander had insisted on bringing her—to have his petty revenge on her by thrusting his very accomplished, very smart, very beautiful ex in her face.

Or was he already regretting his decision to *save* Ani, as he put it? Did he wish he'd stuck to Diana instead? Would he ever tell her why he'd so readily jumped in to help her?

She'd never let a man close for this exact reason and it had always worked. But with Xander, all her usual practicality took a flaming jump out the window, leaving her at the mercy of her foolish heart and frisky hormones. Once, she'd been crushed by his sudden remoteness toward her. Even the warning that she couldn't go through that again didn't stop her from reading more into his actions.

In a dark gray suit that made his eyes pop, Xander looked nothing like the rest of the fuddy-duddy old bankers around. And now, there was an extra element to her attraction to him because she knew what pulsed beneath the suave, ruthless exterior. He'd mentioned his mother with that clinical lack of emotion, and yet he'd done it because he wanted her to know that he understood. Somehow, despite Thea and Sebastian knowing her much better, *he* had seen her wound. His kindness had always had a cruelty to it, but it also had a blistering honesty and zero calculation to it that she appreciated in a life full of broken promises.

Her mama had promised to come back for her, hadn't she? It was why Killian had fought Niven for custody of her for so long, because their happiness together had been tainted by how she'd abandoned Ani to her father.

If Xander made a promise, though, he'd keep it. The more time she spent with him, the more she was caught up in her own silly hopes that took the vague shape of a future she couldn't have. It was like living in the shadow of a huge predator's wings, not knowing when you might be gobbled up but kind of looking forward to it anyway, because at least then it was completely out of your hands and you realized too late that you had a thing for monsters who would bare their own underbelly to protect you.

A sudden burst of raucous laughter from the open terrace made her turn. It was exactly her type of people up there— trophy wives and bored heirs sustaining each other—and she'd had enough of hanging on to Xander like an accessory. Throwing back a glass of champagne on a dangerously empty stomach, she tapped on his arm to catch his attention. When he turned, she snuggled into his side and flashed him a smile, hopefully bright enough to blind him.

"As Diana has pointed out repeatedly, all this talk of international finances is beyond my tiny brain. May I please be excused?"

Of course, snuggling into him to get a rise out of him was a huge mistake because he smelled of woodsy warmth.

"To do what exactly?" he said, leaning down so that only she could see the warning glint in his eyes.

Ani made a pout of her very red mouth—the unrelenting black of her evening gown needed the perfect red lipstick and it made her look hot and sexy and a little wild. "You don't want me to get bored, Xander. That's when the reckless behavior kicks in."

He tapped his thumb against her chin. "Joining that crowd will rein in these…dangerous impulses?"

"Yes, well," Ani said, including a very curious Diana in her reply, "this is the over-thirty-five crowd and all you talk about is making money, and hiding the money you've already made. Out there is the crowd that likes to spend it, like me." She added her signature airhead laugh.

"For a woman who's fixated on wealth and luxury, you keep forgetting to wear half your jewelry," Xander said, pitching his voice low yet again. He ran his finger over the shell of her ear down, down, down the empty lobe. "You didn't like the diamond earrings?"

Ani shivered at the feathery touch, feeling it all the way between her thighs. She clenched them together, desperate for friction. There was something velvety rich and sinful when he spoke like that to her, something very intimate about how he kept their conversation away from prying ears. It was all a web to lure her in and she was inching closer.

She exhaled roughly. "I don't need more presents, Xander. And those are—" she remembered herself just in time "—ancient in design. No one wears huge clusters like that."

He took her right hand in his, where the ruby ring shone brightly. "And yet you don't take this off."

"There's no big mystery to every little thing I do," she whispered against his cheek, desperate for him to drop his relentless probing.

He turned his face until the corners of their mouths touched just so. Air left her lungs in a choppy exhale and she trembled at the effort it took not to meet his mouth fully.

"And yet the truth is the exact opposite, *ne*? I think everything about you is fake. I won't leave you alone until all of this is stripped off, *matia mou*, and you're gloriously bare in front of me."

And then he was the one melding their mouths together for a quick, filthy little kiss that ravaged her to the very depths of her being. It was over before Ani could sink into it.

Xander fixed her lipstick with his thumb, patted her shoulder and said something that sounded very much like "good girl" and then simply dismissed her. And Annika shivered at the fresh wave of arousal blooming between her thighs at his compliment.

Who knew lusting after one's own husband could be so deliciously tormenting?

Xander found Annika close to midnight.

She'd never returned to their table or even to their suite. His mind had been on her constantly. But he couldn't walk out on important people he'd see only once a year because his reckless little wife had broken her promises and was probably out partying somewhere.

It had been a useless exercise in the end because he'd been distracted and irritable all evening. The cold burn of his resentment—at how much she occupied his thoughts—had morphed into something hotter, changing shape and form as the hours wore away. His temper had simmered hot, especially after the phone call he'd received just when he'd started looking for Annika. Especially after Diana had teased him about misplacing his child bride.

All evening, his ex had tried to embarrass Annika several times, reminding him, perversely, why he'd chosen to walk away from a relationship that had been more than a decade in the making. He hadn't stopped her, though, because he wanted to see Annika's reaction, wondered if she'd put Diana in her place. Annika had disappointed him, perversely, by conducting herself just as he had wanted.

With justifiable bitterness after he'd refused to set a wedding date for four years, Diana had made him face the fact that he hadn't considered, even for a second, not showing up for Annika at that church. He was egotistical enough not to like how it painted him and ruthless enough to want to control the narrative in his head even when it was clear that nothing about his actions regarding Annika made any sense.

Clearly, he'd decided he wanted Annika however he could get her. His obsession had become far too deep-rooted for him to wonder *if* they somehow could make it work.

He wanted to conquer her spirit, craved her surrender, in a way he'd never wanted anything in life. She distracted him no end, made him wonder about things he'd never even considered before, drove him to be at the mercy of his emotions, opened him to a bunch of ridiculous notions he'd done well without for this long in his life.

And yet, all the unpalatable realizations in the world didn't stop him from chasing her down.

He found her in the massive ballroom of the hotel that had been newly renovated but was not open to public yet. No doubt one of the younger men he'd seen flit around her had snuck her in here, hoping to inhale a bit of her wildness.

Huge chandeliers hanging from vaulted ceilings illuminated the vast space, fragments of light caressing the woman sitting in the middle of all of it.

All evening, she'd been a vision in the black velvet dress with its shoelace straps. It had taken everything he possessed not to stare at how the thick, soft fabric hung in a loose neckline between her breasts. How her brown skin shimmered against the luxurious softness with a radiance he wanted to lick up. And the complicated knot her hair had been fashioned into...with each hour that passed, one stubborn wayward lock would fall out of it to kiss her shoulders in a tantalizing invitation. A potent reminder that Annika herself would only behave for so long.

Now, at the stroke of midnight, all of it was undone. All of it unraveled just the way he wanted.

He stood under the huge archway, stunned by the glorious creature in front of him. His blood pounded with a feral possessiveness that no one else would behold his wife like this.

With the velvet pushed up to reveal toned thighs and long bare legs, the disarray of her hair swaying about with each movement of her head, her body bowed forward and swung back, eyes closed. She was in...a delicious delirium of pleasure. A sight unlike he'd ever seen. And that was before the music reached his ears.

How he suddenly envied Sebastian his artistic soul. Even though he was built of logic and rationality and numbers on a cellular level, Xander could still appreciate the haunting melody of the tune, could hear the longing and the ache and the sudden pulse of hope fracturing the melancholy.

At the center of the vast black-and-white marbled floor, with the cello between her legs, his wife was lost to the world. Lost in the acute pleasure she weaved with her fingers. Here was the real Annika.

He was standing in front of her when she finished with quite the flourish. Musical notes seemed to soar through the air long after she was done, vibrating with a rich intensity he'd never forget.

Slowly, Annika opened her eyes and looked around, like a baby bird waking up from a trance. Tiny dots of sweat pearled over her upper lip and neck. Her slender arms were trembling when she pulled the bow up and away from the instrument. Reaching down, Xander took the bow and put the cello away.

Sudden tension gripped her shoulder blades as she gathered the thick mass of her hair and bound it into a knot at the top of her head. Her chest rose and fell, the soft little pants of her breaths a new beat to which he automatically tuned himself.

Xander sank to his knees in the space the cello had occupied, loath to let her run away. Loath to let her hide all over again.

Her brown eyes widened into large pools, her palms descending to her belly.

"You play beautifully," he said, knowing that his words were inadequate. Knowing that, despite the desire arcing between them, all he wanted was to delve into her mind. Into her heart even.

"Thank you," she whispered, a slight huskiness to her voice. "Is the interminable dinner over?"

"Why do you hide such talent?" he asked, ignoring her second question. "Such passion?"

"Because the music is mine. My own. Not to be…" A defensive note crept into her words. She looked down, and it struck him that he'd never seen her so…unsure of herself. So vulnerable, of all places, in her perfection. "It was my companion when I lost everything. It is my love, my only love. And love becomes weakness in the eyes of men like you."

Hurt was a jagged thrust through his chest. "You think I would use it as a bargaining tool?"

She shrugged, though a sliver of doubt entered her eyes. "Did you know that once women were forbidden from playing the cello?"

He raised a brow, waiting, knowing instinctually that something lay beneath her anger and aggression.

"By men, who else? With the way the instrument sits between your thighs, and the posture when you play…they thought it might do things to us that our tiny little brains and bodies couldn't possibly handle."

"Ahh, of course. Shall I tell you a secret, though?"

"What?"

"I'm glad you don't share it with anyone, then. Maybe I'm as controlling and ruthless as you say."

"What do you mean?"

"Your music, I would share it with everyone, Annika. But the way you look when you play…"

Her hands moved to her bare thighs then, her fingers

playing with the hem of that velvet dress. Baring another inch of silky soft brown skin. Tantalizing. Taunting. Tempting. "This is nothing, Xander. I've worn much more scandalous things."

He smiled then, because she had no idea how glorious she was and that too was another revelation. "But it is not your body I wish to hide. It is you in that moment, how you look, how you feel, the heart of you that you bare when you play, that I would not share with another man. You're gloriously lost, as if the music itself was moving through you, pleasuring you, provoking you, pushing you to the edge of...everything."

"That's exactly how I feel," she said, worrying her lower lip between her teeth. Then her gaze touched his features, searching. Frowning. Seeking. "I didn't think you'd understand it."

"We're both full of surprises, *ne*?"

"Pity it's not for you to decide who would see me," she said, the fight returning to her. "Maybe tomorrow night I'll play for everyone. Scandalize everyone and cause you displeasure. That would be a nice break from the monotony."

He refused to react to the bait; it was but another distraction to divert him away from the real her. Every conversation with her was a game and he was determined to win. "Did the young fool who brought you here watch you play?"

"No. He...was disappointed, I think."

"Maybe because you were too tired to keep up your act?"

She raised one shoulder.

"Tell me something more about your music."

Surprise flickered in her eyes. "I learned for myself. I play for myself. It is the one thing that I allow myself to weave dreams around."

He realized, then, how truly similar they were. How they both avoided emotional connections for their own reasons. "Your mother used to play it, *ne*?"

She stilled, as if he'd taken a stick and probed at her deepest wound. The hard swallow at her throat made tenderness sweep through him. "You remember? How?"

He hesitated, just for a second. But if the topic he loathed with a bone-deep aversion was the thing that would build a bridge to Annika in this moment, then he would do it. He'd already done it once. This was madness, this thing between them, and for now, he would let it guide him because he wanted the prize. He wanted her enough to break a lifetime's conditioning. And that realization sent a shiver of dread down his spine. But not enough to stop him. "My mother," he said, and wondered that he hadn't choked on the word when he hadn't said it in more than two decades, "used to be supremely jealous of her talent."

"I probably shouldn't have touched that instrument. But it was…irresistible." She met his gaze, hers filled with some inscrutable emotion he couldn't pin down. That familiar, naughty smile found its way to her mouth again. And he saw it then, the artifice of it. "So be prepared to get thrown out on account of being the one who brought me here."

"They won't dare complain. And if you want to play that instrument again, or if you just want it, you can have it."

She laughed and some of the tension arcing between them scattered. Only some, though. "They won't, Xander. I'm telling you, they might even——"

"I'm telling you that if my wife wants that particular cello, she will have it."

Her laced fingers remained on her belly and Xander saw that for the shackle it was. She wanted to touch him but was fighting it. "I…guess that's one benefit of being married to Alexandros Skalas. Even the starchiest, most powerful bankers bow to you."

He shrugged. Power had only ever been a matter of survival to him. It was the only currency his father had understood and appreciated. Once Xander had had a taste of it, he'd held on to it, though. Just like another suit in his closet or a set of cuff links.

Now it pleased him enormously that he could make every dream of Annika's come true with the flick of a finger. *Most of her dreams*, anyway. Though he still wasn't sure if he believed what she'd told Thea that morning.

"You sent every single dollar of my wedding present to your stepfather," he said, bringing up the little nugget that had been eating away at him for hours.

Her smile disappeared. "You're spying on me now?"

"It's a large amount of money to transfer from a joint account, Annika. An alert would obviously go up."

"As your girlfriend pointed out, I'm close to illiterate in these matters." She straightened, her prickliness returning. "I'll ask Sebastian to teach me a few tricks going forward."

Just like that, his own even temper, which was hanging by a thread, vanished. "You will not ask Sebastian for anything. And I mean *anything*."

"You can't just forbid me, Xander."

"Actually, I can. That's the very basis of our agreement, *ne*?"

"Then what if I demand that you stop exposing me to that…woman? I should win a bloody crown for sitting through her condescending lecture while she batted her eyelashes at you and flirted with you relentlessly."

"You sound jealous, *yineka mou*."

"Even a fake wife would be jealous. If I'd poured that champagne down her cleavage, no one at that table would have found fault with me. I'm supposed to be your young airhead trophy wife, remember?"

"You are no airhead, but yes, you behaved remarkably well despite the provocation tonight. I believe in rewarding good behavior. You will have your diamond-studded crown tomorrow morning."

She gasped and her lovely, lush mouth fell open and Xander felt the most overwhelming urge to press his mouth to hers, to swallow her lies and taste her truths and everything in between.

"Now let's come to the real matter. All these years, the money you took from Thea, from Sebastian, you've been sending it to Killian. Why?"

"You don't know that," she said, shifting restlessly. Ready to push him away.

"I want the truth, Annika."

"And what? I'm supposed to hand it over to you, just like that? Because you demand it?"

"If you insist on perpetuating this…act, you will lose. I always get what I want."

"Fine. If you answer my questions, I will answer yours."

"Ask me then," Xander said, holding her gaze.

CHAPTER EIGHT

"Do you wish you'd married her?"

Ani hated the shape and sound of those words the moment they were released. It wasn't the question she meant to ask at all. She sounded needy and clingy and far too invested in his relationship with his ex, but thinking of her mother always left her a little shaky and vulnerable and unsure of herself. She felt lost in the very games she played and Xander was becoming the solid thing to hold on to.

His gray eyes gleamed perceptively. And ever the ruthless strategist, he withheld his answer for long, unbearable minutes.

Ani tried to shift the tension building up around them, but it was impossible…with him kneeling right in front of her. It was a sight she wouldn't have been able to conjure in her wildest dreams. But now she felt a strange blood-thirstiness she didn't understand.

Here he was now, jacket gone, shirt unbuttoned to his chest, hair rumpled, and on his knees—for her. If it was a weapon he was deploying—the soft charm, the gentle probing, the compliments and the interest—it was working only too well. Every inch of her trembled at his proximity, every cell in her wanted to bow toward his solid, enticing warmth.

For the first time in a long time, Annika wanted to make

a choice for herself. Not to fight her stepbrother, not to help Killian and not to feel connected to a mother who had abandoned her a long time ago. She wanted to know that she could still feel something, to give in to pleasure and oblivion and escape, to indulge herself with him. In the end, this thing between them would win. *Xander* would win.

She'd rather choose the time and venue of her defeat, make it a claiming, not a surrendering. And when it was all over she'd walk away, happily owning her desires and needs. She'd walk away, head held high, knowing she'd taken a chip off Alexandros Skalas's legendary control.

"You agreed to answer my questions," she said, feeling her desire flex its claws with the heady urgency of a decision made. The evening scruff on his jaw, his long fingers, the tiny scar near his upper lip, the corded column of his neck...every little thing about him sharpened into focus.

"I broke it off because I felt no urgency whatsoever to meet her at the altar."

"She clearly still wants you."

"I don't want her, *pethi mou*."

Their gazes met and held, his unspoken declaration lying there between them.

"I have one more," she said, leaning forward, both because she wanted to and because she needed to distract him. Her mouth hovered a few inches over his, their breath meeting and melding.

The gray of his eyes deepened. "You're trying to distract me."

"Is it working?"

"Last question then," he said, tweaking the tip of her nose as he used to do a long time ago.

"I want another wedding present."

He laughed then. Head thrown back, tendons in his neck stretched taut, he was breathtakingly gorgeous. And she wanted a bite of the feast. No, she wanted to glut herself on him.

"One more wedding present for Kyria Skalas," he said, grinning.

Annika stared, because she'd never seen him smile like that. Not even as a teen, when he didn't have the weight of the entire world on his shoulders.

"Don't get shy now."

"I want a kiss. No, I want a thousand kisses and I want you." The words rushed out of her. "I want it now." She dragged the tip of her finger down his Adam's apple, the hollow of his throat, down, down, down to his chest.

He stared at her, shock flickering in his eyes. "If this is part of some *game* to control me, Ani—"

"It's not. Everything else in my life…" She swallowed the words that wanted to rush out too—the bitterness, the loneliness, the grief and the fear. "Yes, but not this, Xander. I wouldn't do this for any other reason." She licked her lips and his eyes tracked the movement. "I want this. With you."

Annika had no idea if he moved forward, or if she'd bowed but their mouths met in a frenzy, like starving animals.

She had no thoughts or enough brain cells left to catalog the assault of his tongue licking into her mouth, his teeth nipping at her lips, or the way his long fingers cupped the base of her neck, tilting her mouth this way and that as he ravaged her. Each kiss they had shared until now had been the tip of an iceberg. No, the tip of a volcano. They were chaste, mere pecks compared to this…explosion.

His hands—his large, abrasive-feeling hands—moved

up her thighs, pushing the hem of the velvet dress higher and higher, and his mouth moved from her lips to her jaw to her neck to the pulse fluttering madly there and then he scraped those teeth against her shoulder.

Annika jerked at the jarring pinch of pain and the sweet, sharp pangs of pleasure that followed when he licked the spot. She had no idea how she was breathing. All she could hear was a mad, deafening rush in her ears, a pulsing wave building, one beat at a time, into a torrential tempo, and still, she was left wanting.

"Please, Xander. More."

She felt his laughter like vibrations through her own body, as if she were a tuning fork he operated. His mouth moved from her shoulder, back to her neck and then down her chest. It rankled that he still was in control when she was already in tatters, so Ani grabbed the straps of her dress and tugged the bodice down. A cool breeze kissed her bare breasts.

With her eyes closed, every other sense amplified. The scent of Xander's subtle cologne. The utter stillness of air around him. The rough grunt of his exhale. The tightening dig of his fingers over her inner thighs.

Opening her eyes, Annika reveled in the feral hunger etched on his features, the harsh pants of his breaths. Whatever else he might think of her, this was real between them. Here, they were equals. Here, there was only truth.

His gaze moved from her plump nipples to her aching breasts, to the small tattoo she had gotten under her right breast, to the diamond stud at her belly button, and then back up all over again.

She waited, her heart lodged in her throat, for him to

do something. Anything. For a second, she feared that was merely a game for him.

The hard swallow at his throat brought her breath back into her lungs in a shallow rush. She grabbed the edges of the bench and straightened her spine, faking a brazen sexuality that felt instinctual. His words about not letting anyone see her play—both a warning and a claiming—gave her courage.

For she'd never thought much of her body, her face or even her sexuality. She'd barely even understood what womanhood meant before her stepbrother had tried to turn her into a shiny package to sell to the highest bidder. So she'd done what she had to do. She'd turned her beauty, her body, even her sexuality into a tool. "Maybe you don't like what you see, *ne*?" she said, throwing a husky laugh to cover her floundering confidence. "Maybe you want to return the goods you bought for a refund? Maybe all of this is nothing but a powerful man patching up his ego because he lost to his twin for the first time in his life?"

"If you refer to yourself as goods again, I will take you over my lap and give you a spanking." Then he bit her lower lip in sweet punishment. "Same if you mention him again."

Ani leaned closer, her nipples grazing his chest, all of her being pulsing at that grazing contact. "What the hell do you want from me, Xander?"

"More."

She shivered at the resolve in that one word. "What else is left?" She bit back the sob that wanted to break through. "I've stripped myself bare, literally. Do you want me to beg? Is that it?"

"Your body is a weapon, *ne*? I'm beginning to see your

patterns now. I want more than all the fools who lost their wits over you."

Ani stared, shaken yet again by his perceptiveness. Shaken by his supreme arrogance that she wouldn't just walk out on him. Did he know her desires better than she herself did? "Spell it out for me, then."

"Admit that you've wanted this." He touched her nipple in a quick lash of his tongue that went straight to her sex. "That you've wanted *me* for a long time."

"So all of this," she said, pulling the shroud of her tattered dignity around her nakedness, "is just an ego game to you?"

"You're the one who made it a game, Ani. I'm just making sure I win it."

"Why isn't this enough?"

"Because I want it all. All of your dirty secrets. All of your deepest wishes."

"Fine. Yes, I've been panting over you like a dog in heat for a long while. I kissed you that day knowing it was you. I've never wanted another man like I want you. I've never been this..." Her breath fluttered in her throat, blocking the confession that would shred the little armor she had left.

"Show me how you like to be touched." Leaning forward yet again, he closed his lips around her nipple, leaving it decadently wet, leaving her wet in more places. "Even better, make yourself come."

A lick of a shiver went down her spine. Of course he wasn't going to make this simple or easy for her. This was Xander. Everything was a challenge to be conquered.

She was a prize to be won, she thought with sudden clarity. And she dared not wonder how he'd throw her away when her surrender rendered her appeal stale.

"I've never made myself come," she said, truth making her voice shiver. "That day on the flight, I tried, but…"

"But your lovers have, *ne*? Show me what you like."

Ani felt a flicker of doubt about the wall of lies she'd surrounded herself with falling away at his feet. But if she spilled the truth now, the magic of the moment would disappear. He'd ask more questions and her courage would be gone and she wanted this…*needed* this for herself. "You're being a bastard."

"Because I want to know what you like? Because I want to make sure you remember no one else's touch but mine?"

"Xander—"

"I don't want an act. I don't want the fake Annika you show the world. I want the real you," he said, all steely command in a velvety voice.

Ani laughed, because the other choice was to cry. She'd spun her lies so well and for so long that her truths were not recognizable anymore. This was the real her—the one that had never had a single sexual experience except the kiss she'd stolen from him. The one who hadn't explored her body or her needs, or wondered about the normal, carefree life she was giving up because to do so would open a floodgate she'd kept tightly locked. Because to do so was to face a fear that maybe her heart had been irrevocably broken and she'd never use it again.

The only man for whom she'd broken all her rules was Xander.

Gray eyes held hers in an all-or-nothing dare.

And maybe this was the freedom Xander would give her, she thought, shaking inside. In this fake relationship, she could explore her desire and provoke his and experience everything she'd denied herself. Even risk whatever it was she'd become when he was done with her because his fascination with her was only temporary.

Under his watchful gaze, she lifted trembling hands and cupped her breasts. They were soft and heavy in her palms and ached for a firmer touch. For a rougher clasp. For the expert graze of teeth.

"You are a good girl here, then," he said, such wicked light in his eyes that she thought she might bare and strip every inch of her pride and vulnerability if he smiled at her like that.

"Only here," she said, determined to match him word to word. "And maybe only for you."

An unholy light dawned in his eyes, morphing the gray from a cold flatness to a shining warmth. And she realized that in his own roundabout way, Xander was giving her back all the power and agency that had been stolen from her. That he was pushing her to make her own choices, and for that alone, she'd adore him for the rest of her life.

"Touch me," she said eagerly and then shook her head. "Kiss me, here," she said, rubbing the pads of her thumbs over her peaked nipples. With his gaze on the movement, fire licked through her. "I want to feel your tongue. Your teeth. Your…stubble rasping against me." She pinched the tight buds and nearly came off the bench at the twang shooting to her pelvis. Her moan was loud and brazen and so very needy.

And just like that, he was there. His mouth was there. Licking and swirling and playing with her nipples with such expert skill that she grabbed his hair to hold on and to keep him. His mouth devoured her, alternating between her breasts, releasing her flesh with a popping sound that was a spark at her core. She rocked into his caresses, writhing on the bench, rubbing her thighs together for friction.

Then his fingers were tracing the tattoo she'd gotten under her breast of a cage and a tiny bird fleeing it. "You're a contradiction I will untangle," he said, almost to himself.

Annika swallowed, her brain figuring out how to make words, anew. "No more questions, Xander." Grabbing his palm, she pressed it to her chest, her heart pounding under it. "Or I'll figure out a reason to stop. And I don't want to stop tonight." A near sob filled her voice. "I don't even want to leave this ballroom."

"More conditions, *pethi mou*?"

"You said you'd grant me whatever I ask for."

"I don't have protection."

"I'm on the pill and I'm clean."

"So am I."

Then he was kissing her and lifting her and whispering filthy promises against her mouth. With a surprised laugh, she wrapped her legs around his waist. The tight clench of his abdomen dug into her pelvis and Ani abandoned herself to it. Her breasts rubbed against the soft nap of his shirt but it wasn't enough.

She needed skin-to-skin contact.

She needed his hands over every inch of her flesh.

She needed everything because she wasn't sure she could have this again. Already, she liked Xander's kisses, his touch, his filthy promises all too much. This was already changing her because she already wanted their next time before this time was even over, before this time had even begun.

She squirmed when her back hit the firm upholstery of the chaise longue. And then he was there, his knees straddling her hips, his saturnine face revealed in full glory as he looked down at her.

Pushing up, she unbuttoned his shirt and ran her palms over the hard contours of his chest, the sprinkling of hair, over the tight pack of muscles in his abdomen, back up, up, up over his shoulders, and still she couldn't get enough. She sobbed, feeling an urgent emptiness between her thighs.

His fingers tightened over her roaming hands, arresting their frenzied exploration. Leaning down, he trailed kisses over her neck, her chest, and then his mouth licked at her breast again, suckling, sending sharp pleasure to pool down in her lower belly. Ani was panting and moaning and whining, begging for more, demanding more.

"What else do you want from me, *agapi*?" he asked, his voice sharp with a frenzied edge.

"I want your mouth," she said, licking her tremulous lip, meeting his dare head-on. Meeting herself head-on for the first time. Holding his gaze, she kicked her dress off. Heat poured through her as his gaze swept over her belly and her sex. She cupped herself over the flimsy thong, the tips of her fingers digging where she needed him. "Here. I want your mouth here. No one's ever gone down on me and—"

He didn't let her finish. With one tug, Xander ripped her thong and he was there, on his knees, his proud head bent, his thick hair tickling her inner thighs. He nuzzled the fold where her thigh met her hip, breathing in her arousal, fingers tracing the shape of her most intimate folds.

Every breath inside Ani stilled. The first stroke of his tongue was a feathery lash, gone before she could process it. And then he notched his nose at the tip and licked her again and again, thrashing a rhythm out of every nerve ending, building her to a frenzy. She pushed herself up onto one elbow, dug her fingers into his hair and tugged his head this way and that, a race car driver exploring a new loop. His laughter against her folds was as arousing as the clever assault of his mouth.

Breath serrated, she watched as he looked up. She pulled his hair harder, saw his nostrils flare, and said, "More. Faster. Harder."

He grinned, and then he was sucking at her clit.

Ani lay back, every inch of her writhing and thrashing at the building frenzy, and then exploded, fragmenting into a million shards, flying up and away from all the things that continued to tether her and bind her and keep her lost, even to herself. She wanted to keep flying away on wings of sensation but all of the shards came back together to re-make her. Sobbing, hands searching madly for purchase, she found his steely strength.

Tears on her cheeks, Annika thought maybe being teth-ered was not a bad thing if she could feel such pleasure, if at the end of that spiral and the flight and the crash, Xan-der was there, waiting for her.

Holding her through it.

Looking just as he looked right then, his lips damp with her arousal, his hair rumpled, nostrils flaring and his eyes... those gray eyes alight with emotions she'd thought him im-possible of feeling.

She pushed up and took his mouth in a hard, fast kiss, tasting herself on his lips. She trailed kisses down his jaw and his throat, licked the hollow of his neck, raked her fin-gernails down his chest, drew more kisses from his chest down to his abdomen, following the trail of hair thicken-ing and disappearing under the seam of his trousers. She didn't hesitate though this was new ground.

Undoing his trousers, she snuck her hand inside with a confidence she didn't know she had. Her breath stuttered out of her in a sharp hiss as she touched his hard flesh. His entire body stiffened. Gasping, she ran her fingers over the velvety length of him as if he were the instrument now and she was determined to be the virtuoso.

Renewed hunger filled her as she slowly, instinctively, wrapped her fingers around him.

Xander grunted, dipping his head between her breasts in what felt like a prayer.

Pleasure shot through her in thick, dense pools as she swirled her fingertip in the wetness she found at his tip. Her mouth falling open, she rubbed the base of her palm against it. His exhale coated her breasts and he bit down on her flesh. She jerked as the slight pain contrasted lazily up against the pleasure already simmering through her.

His lashes flickered up and down; his breath was rough, fast pants. She watched every nuance of his reaction to her actions, a strange new power surging through her.

She fisted him, up and down the thick length, feeling fresh dampness at her own core. Leaning into him, she licked the corner of his mouth, feeling a languorous unraveling inside her, as if all boundaries had been broken. She laid open-mouthed kisses over his lips. "I want you inside me, Xander." She bit down on his lower lip, like he'd done to her, intent on marking him. Intent on stealing whatever she could of him. Intent on changing him. "I want to be taken and owned and possessed until I forget how we got here. I want everything you can give me and we'll call this—" another rough stroke of her hands and another grunt from his lips "—the final wedding present?"

He caught her lips with his, with a rough growl that sent

fresh tremors curling through her. On the next breath, he was lifting her until she was straddling him on the chaise longue, and for the flicker of a moment, fear shuddered through her.

She trembled violently.

Straightening up, Xander covered her flesh with his hands, stroking her, soothing her, whispering endearments that brought tears to her eyes. With a brazen strength she dredged up from some sweet, naive corner of her heart, she pushed onto her knees and shook out her hair, so that it fell in waves over her shoulders, the ends kissing her breasts.

He played with the thick, silky strands, strumming her breasts and belly and her sex. "You are beautiful, *matia mou*, and I have wanted to see you like this for a long time."

"You hated me," Ani said, fighting the pleasure his words brought, and failing.

"I hated how much I wanted you," he said with brutal honesty.

"And now?"

"Now you're mine to look at. To touch. To kiss. To ravage and ravish."

"And here I thought Sebastian was the artist in the—" With a gasp, she pressed her hand against her mouth.

"Now you're learning my rules."

For the first time in her life, Ani liked the lush voluptuousness of her breasts, the symmetry of her features, the toned length of her thighs, the soft curve of her belly. She liked the pleasure it brought her—and him. She liked who she could be in these mad moments with him. She almost broke at the thought of who she could be in the future with him if this marriage were real. But that way lay nothing but exquisite hope and enormous pain.

"Will you make me wait now too?"

He shook his head and with one arm cupping her hip, he positioned her as he wanted her and then he pushed up into her in one single thrust that almost cleaved her in two.

Ani gasped as pain ricocheted through her, and before she could catch another breath, he'd turned them both over onto the chaise longue with strength she didn't understand. One tear fell over her cheek and a rough thumb wiped it away. Lower in her pelvis, she felt another rough pinch and suddenly, she felt as empty as she'd always been. And as alone.

She opened her eyes to find Xander standing over her, the shape of his thick erection pushing against his undone trousers, his face wreathed in lines of fury, his gray eyes filled with betrayal.

CHAPTER NINE

XANDER HAD NEVER seen a more beautiful sight than Annika lying on the chaise longue. Hair thoroughly rumpled, her eyes full of lust, her skin shimmering with a damp sheen, her limbs and full curves naked, she was a glorious image he'd remember if he lived to be a hundred. Sharp cheekbones dusted with pink carried lone tears into the dip of her throat, and down into the valley between her breasts.

She looked achingly innocent and thoroughly ravished and…unraveled at his hands.

His entire body felt like one shrieking mass of agonizing, pent-up desire, demanding finish. The sensation of velvet heat clutching him before she—

How could she be a virgin? He'd rammed into her like an animal! Already, her cry haunted him.

Fury and betrayal vibrated through him in twin flames. She'd made a villain out of him, a man not unlike his father. But even if he could live with that, he loathed that he'd caused her pain, that he'd hurt her when it could have been avoided, and that even now it took every inch of his tattered self-control not to take what she so foolishly offered.

Her lies, her acts…it felt like the ground had been pulled out from under him and that was a boundary he couldn't let anyone cross. Not even Annika, for whom he was breaking most of the tenets he lived by. This was supposed to be about getting her out of his system, not letting her lies and truths get to him so much that it robbed him of clarity and control.

Still, desire and something that tasted like a dangerous longing muddied his head, and he couldn't allow that. Unlike his twin, Xander didn't dare test where his boundaries lay. He didn't dare let her cross his control, for he was so much more like Konstantin than Sebastian had ever been.

She extended a trembling hand toward him and every cell and sinew in him wanted to reach out and take it. "Xander?"

"Dress yourself," he said, his words coming from some cold place he loathed.

She licked that full bow of her upper lip, confusion clouding her eyes. "You're stopping?"

He scoffed and it hurt every muscle in his face. "The trail of tears running down your cheeks tells me it is the wisest course of action."

"No, please. I want this. More than anything I've ever wanted in my life."

"Then you shouldn't have played games with me. I told you I hate losing."

Her brow cleared. "You can't just…leave me like this. You promised you'd give me whatever I asked for."

"You're so full of lies that even you have forgotten the truth!"

She smiled then, through tears. With her eyes red, her nose blotchy, her mouth trembling, she reminded him of the girl he'd once adored. "You wouldn't have believed me if I told you the truth."

"I wouldn't have touched you if I had known you were—"

"And there's the alternative that I didn't want. But I guess I underestimated how much your control means to you." Something blazed in her eyes and she pushed up to a sitting position. He saw the grimace she tried to hide from the small movement.

Instinctively, he leaned down to pull her up but she jerked away from his touch, her chin set at that stubborn angle he knew so well.

His gaze swept to her thighs and the streak of pink there. Bile rose in his throat. Picking up the dress, he threw it at her. She didn't lift a hand to catch it and the velvet dress pooled near her feet. "For the past few years, you have loathed me. You judged me because you thought I was a greedy, selfish thief, an airhead flirt, a scandalous party girl, and now…you flip the script? Now what, I'm too virginal for you? Too pure and inexperienced for you?"

"I don't care about that. I care that you spin and weave lie upon lie so that I don't know who you are."

"I didn't know you vetted your sexual conquests with such thorough criteria."

He flinched. "You're not just anyone, Annika." The words poured out of him on a wave of emotion he couldn't understand, contradicting the very order of his thoughts.

She smiled but there was no humor or joy in it. "I'm the girl you hated for years and now I am your wife. How does my virginity change anything?"

He thrust a rough hand through his hair, a tightness pressing down on his chest that he could not dislodge. He hadn't cared how many lovers she'd had in the past because their arrangement had made her his in a way he'd needed.

What he couldn't tolerate was the guilt that pricked him at how he'd spoken to her for years, how he'd thought her beneath him, how he'd used all her tricks as a reason to dislike her. He'd never thought himself a good man—far from it—but a fair man, yes.

All the scaffolding he'd used to build his opinion of her was based on her lies and now it had come toppling down. He felt…disturbingly unsure of what he was doing. Of what—and how much—he was feeling. And he hated that kind of uncertainty, which came with not knowing his own mind.

She'd sent every dollar of her money to her stepfather.

She played cello with a depth of feeling and intensity he couldn't fathom.

She'd never been intimate with a man, despite three broken engagements and a host of scandalous rumors attached to her.

What isolation and artifice and loneliness that must have brought…

She dreamed of love and freedom and a life free of men like him.

Acid burned through his throat.

Everything he'd thought about her was a lie. And the truth that was forming from all the little pieces he kept discovering…he didn't want *that* Annika.

He wasn't equipped to deal with *that* Annika because she was all innocence wrapped in brazen confidence, fragility masquerading as strength, dreams and wishes warped into lies and acts, and he was a man who didn't, couldn't, have a woman like her. Even temporarily. Even just to sate his lust.

She wanted him—there was truth in that. But he could never let himself be led around by this unfathomable obsession. He'd never wanted something or someone so much that it tested his control. It made him examine his own flaws and he couldn't start now.

"So that's it? You're going to leave me here like this? After demanding that I give you the real me, you're going to punish me for a truth that makes no difference at all?"

"No difference? You chose to lie, Annika."

"And, what? You deserve all my truths and dreams and secret desires? Hell no, Xander. We were friends once and you just shoved me aside like distasteful garbage when I didn't measure up to your insufferable standards. Why the hell do you think I owe you anything? This, you and me, all of this, is a convenient arrangement. An itch we're scratching. Why are you suddenly making this bigger than it is?"

Every question that fell out of her lovely mouth was valid. And yet, Xander didn't have an answer that satisfied him, that could stop him from feeling like he was spinning out of control.

"Please Xander. Don't do this." Even her entreaty was a demand and she'd never looked more beautiful.

But he was caught up in his own head and couldn't find the ground under his feet. It took everything he had in him to walk away from the stricken look in her eyes. From *her*. "I don't want you anymore," he said, leaning into that ruthless edge that scared grown men in boardrooms.

She flinched and he thought there would be a special place in hell for him. Nothing new, then, given his genetic makeup.

"This isn't about me," she said, shooting to her feet, looking incredibly weary. "This is all you, the mighty and powerful Alexandros Skalas. You're a control freak and

I'm the variable you'll never understand. I refuse to be the pathetic, rejected one here. It's your loss."

"It doesn't change our deal, *agapi*," he said, forcing himself to say the word with a casual cruelty that sickened even him. "I'll make sure you get your hands on your fortune. Just continue…your act and it will work out exactly as we planned."

Ani wished she could board a flight to New York and simply disappear into the night. Run into her stepfather's arms and vent about the bastard who'd rejected her with such cruelty. Confide her confusion about the torrent of feelings her husband had unleashed within her.

She did nothing of the sort.

With a brittle smile in place, she got through the next two days of the damned charity gala and she played by the rules so well that every man and woman fluttered around the "young, beautiful Skalas bride." Impeccable manners, easy small talk and graceful, witty anecdotes—she owned everyone at the gala.

The final evening, she wore a neon pink dress that wrapped around her neck and chest in wide straps, leaving a little gap in the center of her cleavage and showing a little side boob.

It was the most daring dress amid a lot of boring blacks and staid navy blues. Instead of straightening her hair, she'd let it air-dry into thick waves and plopped on it the diamond-studded tiara that had shown up on her pillow the morning after his brutal rejection.

All in all, she looked hot—even she had to admit it. The dress clung to her curves, forbade any kind of underwear and dipped so low in her back, leaving the top bare, that if someone stood behind her and peeked, they would be able to see her ass.

Something had unlocked inside her with Xander's brutal rejection. There was freedom in having taken the leap and falling hard, with colorful bruises to show for it. She wasn't wearing the dress to break his rules or toe his line.

And as much as she hated him for it, she felt as if he'd released her from a cage of her own making. Ani before Xander's rejection was different from Ani after.

She'd done all she could to take care of Killian and her brothers, she'd survived Niven's mind games and soon she would emerge out of this…debacle, with her fortune in hand. Now it was time to look after herself. Because the one thing Xander's rejection had taught her was that she deserved happiness and love and a real chance at life.

And whether she'd find it or be able to trust a man with her heart wasn't certain but it was time to start living for herself.

She hung on to Xander's arm for the first half of the evening, nodding and smiling politely. Once she stopped treating it as a chore, she actually found herself enjoying the conversation and the people.

Particularly the company of a man around her age, who was clearly at the gala under his father's sufferance. They laughed, more than once, at a shared grievance about fitting into the molds people decided for them. The more she spent time with him, the more she liked him, for he didn't come on to her even once. He even teased her about the covert glances she kept sending in Xander's direction from the moment she'd arrived at the ballroom.

He was perceptive, her new friend. Of course, Ani couldn't tell him that her husband had not only not returned to their bed, but he had not returned to their suite for the last two nights. Which was the most un-Xander thing she'd ever seen.

Deciding that it was his loss was one thing.

Curbing her curiosity about where he'd spent the nights was another.

Which then led her to spying on what Diana was up to. Thankfully, Diana had maintained her distance from Ani. Not that it stopped Ani from imagining that the reason Diana was maintaining a tactful distance was because she'd spent the night with Xander.

Thankful that the ordeal would be over tomorrow morning and she could go back to hiding at the villa, she spent the last hour chatting with her new friend when a tap on her shoulder brought her head up. They'd been so busy talking about classical music and maestros with such exuberance that Ani hadn't even noticed Xander striding toward them. The momentary reprieve from consuming thoughts about him had lifted her spirits. Maybe one day, she'd go a whole day without wanting to kiss him or kill him.

"Dance with me, Annika."

The command grated but Ani pasted a sweet smile, excused herself and followed him to the dance floor. As if on cue, the string quartet switched to a slow, soft classical cover of a pop tune. Ani swallowed as Xander's hands landed on her bare back and then spread wide.

Tension sprang from every inch of her skin that he touched, from the soft graze of his thighs against hers to the way he watched her, his gaze lingering on her mouth.

And what was the point of this exercise at the last minute anyway? She'd charmed the pants off most of his colleagues, reassuring various powerful and privileged men that the mighty Skalas dynasty had a new, fresh brood-mare guaranteeing heirs to continue the line, establishing Alexandros Skalas once again as the apex predator at the top of the food chain.

"I thought you were too ornery and starchy to dance so well," she said, desperate to deflect the building tension.

To her everlasting shock, he shrugged and smiled. "Sebastian loves dancing. Since our father would not permit him to learn outside, I used to dance with him. We would take turns leading."

The thought of the twins dancing in that ballroom, staid serious Xander with charming, laughing Sebastian, made warmth fill her chest. "You really do care about him." The wonder in her words lingered after the sound of them faded.

He raised a brow. "It's survival more than anything else that binds us."

His answer irritated her. Why was it so important to believe and prove that he couldn't care about anyone? What lay beneath Xander's desperate need for control? He'd discarded her so easily two nights ago—did it prove that he didn't care or the opposite? She was twisting herself inside out pondering the damned question.

"Is this necessary?" she asked, breath hitching in her throat when he swung her with a fluid agility.

"Is what necessary?"

"This. You and me. Dancing." She poked him in the chest. "Continuing this farce. I've done my job and charmed everyone beyond even your expectations. Can't I have one hour to myself instead of dancing attendance on you?"

"Is that what you've been doing for the last two hours, chatting with that young man?"

She glared at him. "We weren't flirting."

"I didn't say that."

"If you must know, he's an interesting guy. I've decided it doesn't hurt to develop friendships with those rare individuals who have integrity. When you and I are through, I'm going to be a very rich heiress and I don't want to keep my life on hold forever."

Irritation flickered in his gaze though he sounded perfectly content. "Long-term planning already, I see."

"I knew you'd appreciate it."

"But the young Neilsen heir knows not to mess with what's mine. Even after."

"That makes me sound like a prized poodle, not a wife. Would you like me to wag my tail and trot after you when you walk out of here?"

He laughed and her heart flipped in her chest. A lock of his hair fell onto his forehead and she pushed it back without thinking.

He stilled and she jerked her hand back. His fingers wound around her wrist, and he brought her palm to his face in a gentle gesture that punched through her. "You look beautiful, but something is different, *ne*? You're… glowing from inside out."

She stared, stunned anew by his perceptiveness. Just because Xander chose not to indulge in emotions didn't mean he didn't understand them. Annika kept having to learn that truth over and over. "Your rejection taught me a good lesson. It showed me that I was the one who chained myself. The freedom that I could and should be my own woman, free from the past, is…exhilarating."

"Ahh… No wonder then that every man here is jealous of my good fortune."

She swallowed at the sudden surge of longing thrashing through her. "Don't do this, Xander."

"Do what?"

"You've already decided you don't want me. So why play games?" She pulled back and stared. "Or is it about your ego? Must you show all these men that you possess what they desire? That you're the victor?"

He rubbed his face against her palm before letting go with a scornful laugh. "I was so angry with you, with your lies, your...act. But it wasn't about duping me, was it?"

"Of course not. None of this is about you."

Another self-deprecating laugh greeted her. Really, he was in a strange mood and Ani felt herself drawn deeper and deeper all over again. "Once, I imagined and even hoped that you, of all people, would understand the things we do to survive."

His gray eyes flickered with dawning understanding. "I do. I would have if I—" His jaw tightened impossibly. Whatever his reason was, it was swallowed up by his infuriating need for control.

"You didn't earn the right to my secrets, Xander. And just when I was beginning to think you had, you pushed me away."

He frowned. "You think I enjoyed hurting you further by walking away? It was necessary."

He sounded so unsettled—which was so uncharacteristic of Xander—that Ani was speechless for a moment. Did he really care that much that he'd hurt her? Did it bother him so much that he'd bought her act so thoroughly? Or did the truth make him face something else?

But she wouldn't, couldn't, afford to read more into his words than was there. Couldn't let him twist her inside out. This was supposed to be about doing a good thing for herself, not losing herself all over again in this temporary relationship, in *him*.

"You left me high and dry. You gave me pain and no pleasure like every other man I've ever known—"

"Damn, but you wield your words with such efficiency!"

"And then you went to seek yours," she burst out, far too gone in her jealousy to control herself.

His mouth flinched. "What?"

"Did you go to bed with her, Xander?"

"And if I did?" he asked, recovering already, silky challenge thrumming through each word. "Would you go back on our deal? Would you walk out on this fake marriage?"

How Ani wished she could say yes, but she'd worked too long and too hard to get here.

She looked up at him and realized he knew the answer. He knew she wouldn't give up her fortune. The truth certainly hadn't set her free; it had only made her more vulnerable to the one man who could crush her heart into so many pieces.

Because, it seemed, after all this time, she cared about Xander's opinion. She cared about him. Maybe it was the remnant of fond childhood memories, maybe because she kept seeing glimpses of the real Xander she'd once adored in his actions. Maybe because she was beginning to realize that, despite his veneer of control and ruthlessness, he had a heart that was capable of so much.

And it was impossible to unsee all that, to unsee all that they could be. All she could hope for was that she'd walk out of this arrangement richer and freer, but without losing herself to him. "I would politely remind you that Thea would not name you chairman if you stray before even two months are up."

"That is your opinion of me, *ne*? And you wonder why I walked away." Scorn dripped from his every word. "You think I would take your virginity, make you bleed and run into another woman's bed? What an understanding wife you are."

Frustration made her words come out serrated and shaky. "I don't know what to think, Xander. You asked for the truth and I gave it to you, and you walked away from that moment with such easy cruelty."

"Whatever else it was, it was not easy."

"It shouldn't have been possible at all," she bit out, anger scrubbing the pain away. She pulled back, refusing to give him any more of her pain. He hadn't earned that either. "So yeah, thanks for the reminder that you will go to any lengths to maintain your control and keep the upper hand."

"You think it was a power play?"

She sighed. "What else can it be?"

"I don't do well with lies. With surprises. With things being out of my control. With things not conforming to the narrative in my head."

Her eyes wide, Ani took in the flaring nostrils, the tic at his temple, the remote bleakness in his eyes. She wasn't sure if she liked that she'd forced him to explain, that she'd clearly caused him some kind of pain. "Is that an apology? Or an explanation? OMG, has the sky caved in yet?"

A smile barely touched the corners of his mouth. "Shut up and dance with me, Ani."

"Why?" Ani said, bracing herself against what his words did to her. Every time he said her name like that, with that possessive pride, she found herself stripped before him.

"Give me one good reason why I shouldn't punch your face in for abandoning me like that, for leaving me to an empty suite for two nights?"

"Because I've been dying all evening to dance with my beautiful wife," he said instantly. "Ever since you walked out in that dress, with that tiara in your hair, looking like a queen. I recognized something about the girl I once knew in that woman tonight."

The husky honesty in his words undid Ani at a new, deeper level. He was telling her he saw her finally without saying it. That he saw her battles, her struggles, her flaws, her acts, that he saw...*her*. Her already flimsy resistance to him crumbled.

Ani was finally understanding how to read him, how she'd read him as a girl a long time ago without the confusion of adulthood. Commanding his wife to dance with him as Alexandros Skalas was different. He wore a mask as much as she did, only his was unyielding, near permanent, and fused into who he had to be in public.

But dancing with her after he'd admitted, without actually admitting it, that he'd been thrown by all the different facets of her was near miraculous.

"I'd love to dance with you," she whispered, afraid he'd hear her deepest dreams if she said them too loud.

He smiled fully this time and it was like a thousand free birds fluttering their wings in her chest. It felt like a beginning and an ending and Ani smiled back, finding the moment, and him, irresistible. And then he was dipping her deep into a dive, his arm tight around her waist. But she felt no fear of falling, only a weightless floating. And he saw that too.

She gave herself over to the tune, to the rhythm and to

him. She lost herself in his tight embrace, in his scent, in the gray depths of his eyes.

He led them around the ballroom with a smooth grace that highlighted the wiry strength in his shoulders, the rock-hard thighs, the innate masculinity of him. But what cast a net around her heart and lured the foolish organ to play once more was his laughter. The pleasure written into his features as she joined in. His hands, his smiles, his moves… they enchanted her, caged her all over again in a new way just when she'd decided she needed to break free.

Applause broke out around them as they finished the dance with a flourish. Flushed, chest rising and falling, Ani looked up to find him watching her with a naked hunger that made her want to sob.

Why didn't he just give in and put them both out of their misery? What kind of a sadistic bastard denied himself what was willingly given and desperately wanted? How deep were his scars that he couldn't let go even in this way?

"Xander—"

"Give me one real thing about you," he interrupted her, dipping his head low until his mouth rested on her pulse. "Willingly."

She shivered at the sudden touch. "What? Why?"

His exhales coated the fluttering pulse at her neck, his fingers drawing lines over her spine. He was seducing her will away from her one word, one caress, one question at a time and he didn't even want her. No, he *wanted* her. He'd just decided he couldn't have her, for some ridiculous reason.

"Because I want to know you, Ani."

Ani… Somehow, his use of her nickname felt intentional, making a joke of the warnings in her head. "I'm tired. I would like to go to bed, please," she said, fighting the lure. But there was something in his tone—a need wrapped in a command—that made her pause.

He pulled back, his gray searching hers with a sudden urgency. "What would make you the angriest?"

"Letting my stepbrother win after everything he did to break me," she said. She was giving up a truth she'd never given voice to before, and suddenly, released into the sacred space between her and Xander, it lost its power; its hold on her.

She thought he'd probe and pick at the wound but the only sign that he'd even heard her was his hands tightening on her arms.

"What would make you the happiest?"

Kissing you. Seeing that desire in your eyes for me. Having you move inside me. Having you claim me for real. Belonging to you.

The answer came as easily and naturally as her breath, and it scared the hell out of her—how deep she was already in.

"Seeing my brothers," she said, going for her second choice. "I'd give anything to spend just a few minutes smushing them. They love me like no one else ever has."

She hadn't meant to say it like that, but she didn't regret the words either. She was tired of being afraid and pretending like she wasn't. She was tired of wanting so much and acting like she needed nothing.

His brow cleared as he nodded, then he walked her to their suite, hand resting at her lower back, and left her standing in the middle of the room, staring at his retreating back.

She couldn't help calling out his name. "Xander?"

He turned and Ani saw something she'd never seen in his face before. Ever. Regret darkened his eyes, leaving his mouth with a bitter twist. "Farce or not, I would not look at another woman, much less touch one when I'm married to you, *matia mou*. When I'm consumed by thoughts of you." He tucked his hands into the pockets of his trousers, his gaze touching every inch of her in a tender caress. "Go to bed, Ani."

She nodded, her heart settling from its mad, rabbiting pace for the first time that day. Because she believed him. And now she could sleep without wondering what about her had driven him away.

CHAPTER TEN

ANI AND XANDER returned to the villa in Corfu, and she slid back into the routine of running and playing her cello and hiding from him when he wasn't actively facilitating the distance between them by working. In front of Thea, their strange, wordless truce easily looked like a married couple settling into domesticity. Because even with the distance they both maintained, the charge between them was always there, striking into a conflagration at the most innocent of touches.

It seemed they were in some kind of holding pattern. His polite kindness and his concern for her were more torturous than all the contempt and dislike she'd faced for years.

Three days later, Ani heard the airborne thrum of two choppers. Dressed in tank top and shorts, she rushed to one of the overhang terraces that provided a breathtaking view of the island. The helipad showed four distinctive figures she'd recognize anywhere in the world.

Screaming, Ani ran down the stairs, barefoot, wet hair dripping thick clumps of water down her back. Excitement and joy swirled through her as she crossed the stretch of green that separated the house from the landing pad.

Ayaan, already taller than her by several inches, threw his lanky arms around her and she thought how much he'd changed in just two months. The middle one, Aryan, shyest of all, waited for her to greet him. And the little one, Ayush, handed her a slimy toad as a gift.

Ani tried—and failed—to fight the tears when Killian enfolded her in his arms.

At the familiar scent of his cologne and the solid comfort of his bear hug, a sob rushed out of her. Burying her face in his chest, she cried her heart out, unable to stop her emotional outburst.

The hairs on the nape of her neck prickled and she turned to find Xander on the highest terrace of the villa, watching them. Watching her.

Across the cliff of the mountain, across the distance—it seemed, across the universe itself—their gazes held. His, offering amends, and hers, desperately wanting but unable to reject it.

"What would make you happiest?" he'd asked, and this was the result. Would he give her what she *really* wanted if she asked?

Maybe he deserved her gratitude, but Ani couldn't see her way past the fear in her heart. She knew she hadn't processed all the emotions he'd been unlocking in her from the moment he'd come to save her at the church. She couldn't even offer him a nod.

He was twisting her inside out, and soon there would be no escape.

Cutting her gaze away, she lifted her young brother who instantly scrabbled over her back like a monkey, threw out a dare for a race and took off running while her two brothers kicked up sand at her heels.

She wondered at how her heart could be so full of joy and happiness and still want more. How she could be surrounded by people who loved her and still miss another. Still crave another. Still need another.

"You have given her a wonderful present, Xander," Thea said the moment Xander sat down to breakfast with her, three weeks after Annika's brothers had arrived at the villa.

More like an easy way to relieve his guilt, but Xander didn't say it.

Behind them, on the strip of the private beach, they could hear Annika and her brothers' raucous laughter and shouts. The villa had never been witness to such exuberant joy and antics.

Not even before his gentle mother had started drinking to cope with his father's brutal control. Not even before Xander's hero worship of Konstantin had been shattered when he'd found him terrifying Sebastian with a belt in his hand. Because, of course, Xander had been the perfect son, the perfect heir, the perfect firstborn, desperate for Konstantin's love and approval.

It was only when he'd displeased Konstantin by taking him on in defense of Sebastian that Xander had realized the kind of man his father was and how conditional his approval was. They'd never been an emotionally expressive family even before he'd understood just how broken they were.

It wasn't just Annika's brothers that were responsible for the tangible delight that had been reverberating through the empty walls of the villa.

It was her. She had turned a holiday for the boys into treasure hunts and beach races and hide-and-seek games and scary stories at night and sleepovers and early morning swims and excursions to explore the flora and fauna around the villa.

It was everything he and Sebastian had never known as boys, everything boys should grow up with. Everything Annika would give to her own children when she had a family with the man she loved—a future he could see so clearly now, whatever she did with her fortune.

The thought struck Xander like a fist to his solar plexus, knocking the breath out of him. It wasn't like he could banish her from his life forever after this was over, because she was his grandmother's goddaughter and his twin's best friend and she'd be his...*ex*.

Even if he somehow managed to remove her from his life, Xander had a feeling he'd never be able to purge her from his head. From his—

A sudden scream of laughter had him turning around.

Like an outsider watching through a dirty windowpane, he craned his neck to spot Ani carrying her youngest brother—the one she called Bug—on her shoulders and running into the waves lapping at her feet. She ran in and out, not even a little tired at carrying the boy on her back, endless in her enthusiasm for childish play and adolescent games.

In a hot pink tank top that was plastered to her chest thanks to the spray of water, and cut-off denim shorts hinting at the round globes of her glorious ass, she was temptation incarnate.

In three weeks, her appearance had changed drastically. From the suave, sensuous, perfect Skalas wife to this exuberant woman. She was always half wet, in shorts and tank tops, her hair full of sand, her skin tanned, her lips chapped thanks to the hours she spent with "her boys" down at the beach, exposed to the sea breeze.

She'd never looked more beautiful, for joy had etched itself into her features. And Xander wished he could always see her like that, as she was now, happy and surrounded by love. To arrange the very world to suit her needs.

She'd even bedded down with them on the floor with sleeping bags in Sebastian's wing, claiming Bug didn't want to sleep alone in a strange house.

He should have been relieved that there was no need to resist her every single time he walked into his bedroom. His bathroom counters were empty enough to see the gleaming black marble again, and his bedroom excruciatingly organized without her clutter, and his bed was empty and enormous without her spread-eagled on it.

There was no relief. Only a loneliness he'd never felt in his life before. They hadn't even properly slept together and she was already under his skin. He was running out of reasons why he couldn't treat this as a mutually pleasurable agreement.

It had been a valid question from Annika and he still didn't have an answer—not one that he understood and found acceptable. Because what he wanted was more than scratching an itch. More than the mutually convenient farce he'd planned. And that way lay an impossibility. A specter he didn't want to face. A painfully awful dive toward the deepest fear he'd never let surface before.

"Xander?" Thea prompted.

He rubbed a hand over his face. "I was getting tired of seeing a morose, miserable wife, Grandmama."

"I wish you would let yourself—"

"And I wish you had told me how much she suffered at her stepbrother's hands."

Consternation filled Thea's eyes. "Did she share that with you?"

"I surmised enough," Xander said, helplessness fueling his anger. "How could you leave her there, year after year?"

"He was her legal guardian, Alexandros. Still, I did not give up on her. Still, I fought to have her every summer. Annika is a proud creature. For a long time, even I didn't know how he much tormented her."

"Why not ask me to step in on her behalf?"

"Then I would become another person who takes away her choices, who takes away her power over her own life. She told me she didn't want to bring that misery here, that this was an escape. She is as proud and stubborn as you are, Alexandros. I have done all I could, all she would let me do."

"You suggested she marry Sebastian," Xander said, his mouth turning dry with anger and jealousy.

He'd been blind not to see it before now. Of course it had started at Thea's suggestion—a solution for the two people she loved most. He looked away, loath to let her see the betrayal he felt, the strange loss of something he hadn't even known he valued. It seemed now that if he acknowledged the tiny sliver of emotion he felt for Annika, everything else would flood in.

"I did not think you were right for her," Thea said, unflinching in her brutal honesty, saving him from spelling out his disappointment. "Ani deserves—"

Xander pushed back his chair with a hard scrape and shot to his feet. He knew what his young, innocent, strong-as-fire wife deserved.

One look at her was enough to know it.

Ani was the kind of woman men built families and legacies around, the kind who spawned legendary love stories. The kind who would fight for her love, for her children, against anyone, the kind who would spread sunshine wherever she went. The kind who loved from the very depths of their soul.

Having been a stranger to that kind of love meant he and Sebastian had a better awareness and understanding of what it meant and what it demanded and what it took. And crystal clear clarity about their own capabilities in the matter.

"I have a meeting," he said, and was about to leave when Killian Mackenzie and Ani arrived with their arms around each other.

The older man extended his hand toward Xander, gratitude shining in his eyes. "Thank you for arranging this trip. The boys needed it and I'm thrilled to see Ani so well looked after."

Next to him, his stepdaughter bristled at the comment and Killian laughed. "Don't begrudge me my gratitude, Ani."

"We don't have to prostrate ourselves in front of him, Killian. Arranging the trip is hardly more than a moment's effort for Xander," Annika said irritably.

"Hush, love," Killian said. "I'm sorry we've monopolized her so much. I didn't know until just now when Bug told me that she'd been sleeping by him. The scoundrel was taking advantage of her kindness and I'm sure she could have just—" The already ruddy man flushed, realizing what he'd been about to say. "Thank you, Mr. Skalas, for your generous hospitality."

"Please, call me Xander."

Killian nodded.

"Ani's family is ours too. You're welcome here anytime. All you have to do is call my assistant and she'll set up the flights." Xander was surprised to realize he meant the words. In his few dealings with Killian to ensure the smooth transfer of the funds Ani insisted on sending him, he'd learned of the older man's integrity. Understood the extent to which his business had been run to the ground through maliciously targeted actions taken by Ani's stepbrother.

He understood why Annika had fought for so long against Niven, instead of giving up. This man had given her something even her mother hadn't been able to. As was her nature, Ani was determined to pay back a thousandfold the kindness he'd done her.

The little time he'd spent with her brothers had been enjoyable in a way he'd never known before. Not that her teenage brother had warmed to Xander. Whatever magic Sebastian had spun, Ayaan seemed to be firmly lodged in his twin's camp. Xander felt the most overwhelming urge to win the teenager over to his side. To win all her family members over to his side the only way he knew—by showering them with gifts and lavishing riches on them.

Which was ridiculous because he was a grown man and he didn't even want Annika's good opinion or her trust or anything more. *He didn't*, he repeated to himself.

"I'm glad you seem to know the way to Ani's heart," Killian continued, while Xander could only nod in silence. "It's like she's a completely different person from the Ani I've known all those years," he couldn't help adding.

Only then, finally, after three weeks of evading him, of fake smiles and platitudes in front of Thea, Annika met his gaze. He had no idea what she saw in his but she searched and probed before saying, "This was the best wedding present by far, Xander. Thank you."

The words were stiff, begrudgingly given, and ratcheted up the sudden awkwardness around them, making it tangible enough that his grandmother and her stepfather stared at them back and forth, as if it were a tennis match.

"I hope our presence hasn't created problems for you both. I'd never—"

"Xander and I don't live in each other's pockets. In fact, my husband prefers me not to be demanding and clingy. He prefers me to get my needs met through other means, instead of begging him for attention."

The words landed in the space between them like the gauntlet they were, drawing both Thea's and Killian's attention.

"Behave, Annika. The man let three rowdy, grubby boys invade his home for three weeks. The least you owe him is a proper thank-you. A kiss, even," Killian said, determined to smooth out the ripples between them.

Raising a brow, Xander let Annika see the challenge in his eyes.

Exhaling on a heartfelt sigh, she crossed the distance between them, walking toward him like a martyr approaching the sacrificial pyre.

Her palm on his chest, she went up on her toes to kiss his cheek and something like the very devil stirred inside Xander. He wanted more than a peck offered under sufferance. He wanted everything.

Annika had shown him the shape of a future he'd never imagined for himself even in his wildest dreams. A future he wasn't equipped for.

For the first time in his life, he felt anger and a near painful powerlessness at everything he'd been robbed of by his parents. Of how much he'd lost by molding himself to be what was required. Of how much he didn't know of what it was to… But he wouldn't lose her. He wanted that future she'd showed him and he'd have it through other means, through every strategy available to him.

He turned at the last second so her mouth landed at the corner of his. Palms on his chest, she flinched, but didn't pull back. Sinking his fingers into her thick hair, he tilted her chin up and dusted away the thin layer of sand stuck to her jaw.

Then he bent and kissed her cheek, tasting sand and water and sun on her skin. He tasted joy and desire—everything he'd never known he wanted, much less needed. Even the acrid taste of fear in his throat couldn't stop him from gathering her tight in his arms.

How he'd missed the feel of her curves in his hands, her scent in his nose, her taunts and her digs in his head. "If you've further damaged that tendon in your thigh after your adventures, I'll never invite them again."

Despite his growled threat, she settled into his arms with a soft groan, like a kitten coming in from the cold. "I didn't miss physiotherapy for one day."

"But you've lost weight in just three weeks," he said, feeling a strange tenderness well up inside him.

Her eyes widened, something shifting in her expression. Some of her anger melting away, he thought. "I haven't had an appetite since we returned."

He didn't pick up the gauntlet she'd thrown down. He spoke quietly. "Did you have enough time with them?"

She nodded. "Was that my reward for good behavior?" she asked softly, snuggling deeper into him, as if she meant to stitch herself into his skin. "Bringing my family here? Because I could get used to it."

"Could you?" he asked, tempted beyond distraction to

promise her the world, to bind her to him with some new deal, to control the outcome of this game before she realized he was playing it for real.

What if that was how he was supposed to bind her to him? By using this inexplicable, relentless need between them, by making all her dreams come true...?

Xander calculated the risks, formulated the strategy, and tried to forecast the outcome. Because one thing he didn't know, and refused to even anticipate now, was losing.

Annika nuzzled her face into the hollow of his throat, knowing Xander was only allowing the intimacy for the sake of their audience. She'd missed crowding him in their bedroom, messing up his stuff in his study, missed being near him. She was such a loser when it came to this battle between them—while he probably didn't even consider it one. Or if he did, he believed he'd already won it.

"I could do this for a long time if the perks are this good. I'd have even come to you first instead of going to Sebastian," Ani added, wanting to thrust her own blade in just a little, wanting to see if this misguided distance was taking the same toll on him.

"Believe me, *pethi mou*. I'm well aware of my strengths and my weaknesses in comparison to Sebastian."

For the first time in her life, Ani didn't like the taste her words left behind. She straightened, shame heating her cheeks. "That was an awful thing to say. I'm—"

Xander held fast, refusing to let her pull away. "I can bear the cuts, Ani. You're used to fighting, *ne*? I'm too, for what I want." He palmed her jaw, looking at her as if she were a puzzle he was determined to decipher. "And this wasn't a reward, nor an incentive. Not punishment, not a deal."

She swallowed at the sudden rush of longing those words unlocked inside her. "To assuage your guilt, then?"

Some new resolve shimmered in his gaze. "No. I wanted to see your happiness."

The cello arrived three days later—one of the most expensive in the world, made in the eighteenth century by a master craftsman. It was even more precious than the one she'd unwisely touched at the hotel in Lake Geneva, and a sign from the universe.

So yeah, she didn't need a thirty-million-dollar cello as a sign, but she'd been considering applying to music college and getting a degree when she was finally free. She could practice on it until she wasn't Xander's wife. Treat it as a once-in-a-lifetime treat. Work on her skill. Be ready when this was…over.

For an hour, Annika walked around the cello, afraid to touch it, afraid even to breathe near it, making perambulations like a pilgrim around a temple. But even the awe in her heart at having access to such a beautiful instrument didn't outlast or outweigh the confused ache she felt for the man who'd bought the beautiful instrument for her.

What was Xander doing and why?

He lavished expensive, thoughtful gifts upon her and yet he barely touched her. In the three weeks since Killian and her brothers had visited, he'd barely been home. He'd had her flown out to meet him for a dinner on a yacht in Morocco for one night, where she'd played her role perfectly. Then he'd sent her home with a polite kiss on her cheek. He might as well have given her a gold star for good behavior.

"I wanted to see your happiness."

He'd said it with such determination and deliberation, but would he ever give *them* a chance? And yet, to her the words were magical because no one had wanted to see her happiness like he did. Every inch of her was beginning to believe that this farce was the realest thing in her life.

Fighting tears, Annika finally lifted the bow and drew it across the strings of the cello. The music she created instantly lifted her spirits, infusing her with a feeling of being alive, with courage and desire.

She was crying when she finished playing a while later, her arms and shoulders sore and tight. The instrument already owned a piece of her heart, as did the man who had given it to her. And she herself felt lighter, her mind clearer, free of fears thrust upon her by her stepbrother, or the secret wish she'd nurtured for years that if she was back with Killian and the boys, she'd somehow have her mom back, or the foolish hope that by protecting the boys, she'd somehow earn the approval of a parent who had left her behind.

Acknowledging the truth made her feel powerful. Ready. For the first time in her life, Annika could appreciate what she had and all the things she could have, all the things Xander would give her if she extended her hand. Her heart. It was all within her power.

The only question left was whether she'd dare do it, whether she could survive asking for everything.

Xander returned to the villa after being away for three weeks. The maximum amount of time he could stay away, while still being in control.

Ani had been beautiful and elegant at that soiree on the yacht sailing along the French Riviera, like a glittering gem with all its rough edges finally polished away. But not an act. Something had changed about her, as if she was finally emerging from the cocoon of smoke and mirrors.

When the cello player of the popular string quartet that had been hired to play for the evening had been absent, she'd stepped in. It was her first time playing in public, her first time sharing her music, and she'd shone. Xander had felt a possessive pride to see her up there, to know that she and her music and her wicked quips and her daring challenges all belonged to him.

A good thing he'd drummed it into his head at a very young age that his business trumped everything else, because it had been near impossible to drop her at the helipad.

And in those moments when he'd stood leaning against the car, watching her walk away toward the waiting chopper, with his jacket around her slender shoulders, her face turned over her shoulder, her eyes speaking to his across the distance, he'd known his plan could work, that the biggest risk he'd ever taken would pay off.

CHAPTER ELEVEN

IT WAS PITCH-DARK when Xander arrived at the villa close to midnight, to find it alarmingly silent. He checked his phone to see if he'd missed a call from Thea about a social engagement but there was none.

He undid his tie and rolled back his cuffs as he spotted a sleek figure swimming laps in the overhang pool attached to Sebastian's wing.

Moonlight sprinkled golden dust over long limbs swishing through the water. Reaching Sebastian's floor, Xander poured himself a glass of whiskey—his twin always had the good stuff—and went to sit by the pool. Beyond the pool, a view of the dark sea stretched out for miles, and the scent of wildflowers hung thick in the humid air.

It was a peaceful spot—something he'd never noticed before.

Annika instantly changed direction and swam toward him. With her usually unruly hair plastered to her scalp, the high cheekbones and her wide mouth came into stark relief. Stripped of makeup and all the armor she usually wore, she looked very young. Definitely too innocent for him. Not that it would stop him from taking what she offered. He wouldn't make that mistake again—not now that he knew all of her. Not now that he had a plan.

He could finally see what his actions had communicated when he'd walked away from her that night in the ballroom. Not just a rejection of their intimacy or what had already seeded between them, but a rejection of everything she'd overcome. By treating her as fragile, he'd taken away her power. He'd become just another man who tried to control her.

"I didn't know you were coming home tonight."

Something about the casual, almost welcoming way she greeted him threw him. He looked inside the whiskey tumbler, cursing himself for all the missteps he'd made with her. "Is this home to you, Ani?"

He braced himself for a roundabout, flaky answer. She surprised him, yet again, and he wondered at how he could never be entirely sure he knew what she might say or do. But he liked that about her.

Her eyes glowed as she said, "Its allure dimmed for a while, but not anymore. Whatever happens in the aftermath of this—" she waved her hand between them "—it will always be home to me. Even if I'm not welcome here."

"It worries you that you might not be," he repeated, taking that in. "What would you have done when Sebastian and you separated? Or did you think you could really make the marriage work?"

"Anything I would've had with Sebastian is different from this, with you, Xander. There was never anything more than friendship between us. He helped me out and let Thea weave her fantasy about how the marriage might save him. Which is stupid enough because no one knows if Sebastian needs saving, much less himself."

Xander swallowed another gulp of whiskey, resenting the warmth that crept into her voice when she mentioned

Sebastian. That he had lost her affection through his own actions wasn't lost on him. In fact, it was a pretty big indicator how the future would shape itself, given who he was. But he'd won before in his life, even when the odds had been stacked against him. And he would this time too.

"I changed my itinerary at the last minute," he said, picking up the question she'd asked. "I have to leave tomorrow morning again, though."

She rested her chin on her arms on the lip of the pool, studying him with an intensity she didn't hide. "I don't like staying here when Thea is away. The villa's too quiet and the nearest village too far to walk to."

"Use one of the cars in the garage."

"I don't know how to drive."

He frowned. "You're twenty-three. How can you not know?"

"I've lived in New York most of my life, and I had chauffeurs and bodyguards to drive me when I lived with Niven."

"I will have someone come in to give you lessons."

She pouted. "If I have to learn, I want you to teach me."

Surprise caught him in a chokehold. "That would not be a good idea, *pethi mou*. I'm not known for my patience. We'll be at each other's throats before we even leave the estate."

"Or maybe we'll rip each other's clothes off. I've never done it in a car. Either way, I'll learn something new."

Xander cursed, loud and long, but it didn't dispel the tension building inside of him.

"I'm not a fragile, wispy thing to be scared away by you, Xander. I've faced a real monster. And I—"

"I'm sorry, Annika." He pressed his whiskey tumbler

to his temple, unable to meet her eyes. "I'm sorry that I did not see it."

"Not your fault."

"It is my fault, when you're part of the family."

"More like a hanger-on, you mean. You had no duty toward me, especially when you clearly pushed me away. And I still don't know why."

"Do not look for noble reasons behind my actions, Ani. Hear what they say."

"Not until they tell me what I want to hear."

His mouth dried at all the possibilities she painted with that answer. The minx was luring him in as well as if she were a siren singing her song. "You're stubborn."

"A lot like you. And I always thought we were total opposites."

He smiled then. It was impossible not to when she was in such a warm, playful mood.

"So you do plan to be away this long regularly?"

"I have a few big fires going on right now. Things I need to get in place to convince Thea to make the announcement."

"I never realized how hard you work. Sebastian definitely doesn't."

"Sebastian hates everything to do with the Skalas Bank and the legacy. If he didn't think it would hurt Thea immensely, he would have thrown his share of the pie at a charity a long time ago. Instead, he lets me handle his money and be his proxy in the boardroom."

"And you give him back millions of euros in profit."

"Are you looking for someone to manage your fortune, Ani?"

She laughed then, and he heard a freedom in it he'd

never heard before. As if she'd let go of everything that had weighed her down before. "I'm just trying to understand what your life is like. It's not as one dimensional as I thought."

"Ouch."

She giggled this time and there was no way he could resist it. Resist her. He needed the taste of her in his veins, now. He bent forward from the lounger and caught her mouth with his. She tasted like moon-kissed light and raw, artless desire and the darkest decadence.

She returned his kiss with a fervor he'd come to need as much as her taste. When she climbed out, he brought her into his lap, all the while nibbling away at her sweet lips. Urgency beat at him. Why had he wasted so many days?

He knew the answer, but this time desire beat out everything else.

She laughed against his mouth, drenching him, clinging to him, kissing him, devouring him with her little groans and mewls and demanding nips.

He filled his hands with her curves, need revving through him like wildfire. Her breasts were perfect in his hands, the nipples beading hungrily against his palms. Using his fingers, he pulled down the cups of the bikini top and flicked at the plump knots. She arched into his touch, thrusting them up, and Xander latched his mouth on to one brown nipple. Her raw groan rippled through her body and his.

Water drops from her hair hit him like wet lashes, and he wondered if they were sizzling on his hot, hungry skin. Drawing her deep, he suckled on her breast and she went wild. Her fingers descended into his hair, tugging and pulling, as he lavished the same attention to the other breast.

Then she moved up on him, straddling him until they were locked.

"You're so wet," he murmured against the valley between her breasts, wanting to feel warm, silky flesh.

She giggled, dripping water onto his face, then found his mouth. "I'm thinking it's the bikini you're talking about?"

He grinned too. Their gazes met, and something passed between them, something bigger than them both, an unspoken communication. Almost a communion. And the fiery waif that she was, she didn't shy away from it.

Her hands clasped his cheek. A shaky exhale whispered out as she kissed him softly, tenderly, and Xander thought his heart might punch out of his chest. "If you give me two minutes," she said, rubbing her damp cheek against his mouth, "I'll shower and smell minty fresh."

"No," he said, pulling away the thread of the flimsy bikini around her neck. Her breasts fell into his palms, as did a soft gasp from her mouth as he kneaded the soft weight. "Sebastian fills that damn pool with mountain water. As for you…" Pushing her onto her knees, he pulled off her bikini bottoms. From a table next to the lounger, he grabbed a towel and wiped her down.

He took his time with every curve and dip, touching and licking the flesh he wiped dry, learning every inch of her. A sudden breeze drifted over them and she shivered. He pulled her closer while she busied her fingers with his shirt buttons, sudden tension wreathing her.

"Look at me, Ani," he said, trying to make it a request and failing.

She looked up and he thought he could see her heart in those big brown eyes. He cursed himself for not recognizing the bounty she was all these months.

"You're shaking, *agapi mou*," he said, running his palms softly over the goose bumps on her silky smooth flesh. The words fell easily from his lips.

"I can't take another rejection," she said, on a broken whisper. "You're the only thing I've reached for in my life for myself. Maybe I should've told you that instead of playing games. But my life has been—"

"Shh… Ani," he said, gathering her close. Instead of offering empty reassurances, he ran his thumb down her belly button to the jut of her sex. He played with the swollen bundle of flesh that had popped out of its hood and stood proudly, demanding his attention. He traced every inch of her folds and went further down, notching a finger at her entrance.

Damp arousal flooded his fingers. Damn, but she was ready and so was he. Holding her gaze, he unzipped his trousers and freed his shaft. The mere touch of his own fingers made pleasure surge through him. He notched the tip at her entrance, bathing himself in her welcome wetness.

On her knees, she undulated her spine, leaning in and away so that she rubbed herself against him. Playing with him. Teasing him. Casting a lure so wide and so deep that he thought he might never get out of it.

One hand on her hip, he thrust inside her on one of her downward movements and all the world seemed to cease around them. She gasped and closed her eyes.

Breath serrated in his throat, Xander waited with patience he didn't know he had. He pressed his mouth to the curve of her breast, while sending his hands to stroke down her damp back, wanting to soothe her.

She writhed in his hands, moving forward and back, pulling those hips up and down in tiny movements, testing the fit, learning and chasing her pleasure. It was the most erotic sight Xander had ever seen. "You're a natural at this," he said, catching her lower lip with his teeth.

She sank into the touch and nipped him back. "Nah. I researched it. I just need a little more to get used to you. To this."

He smiled. "Take your time."

Lifting her hands to her hair, she stretched like a cat. "This feels good, Xander. So good. You?"

"It's perfect, Ani. You're perfect."

With every slide and shift and slip of her hips, pleasure raced down his spine like lightning, gathering in his balls. He tightened every muscle in his body against the oncoming spiral, against instincts urging him to move, thrust and pound into her.

"Okay, thanks for your patience. That slight pinch is fading," she said, in a husky voice, rubbing her breasts against his chest, her palms stroking every inch of his taut, muscles. "Now can I have more? All of you?"

He looked into her eyes, his jaw tight, holding on to the last thread of control. "I'll stop anytime you want me to, if it gets too much."

She nodded, pulling farther out of his reach, but he arrested her movement. "I know. Xander, oh, Xander, it hurts not to have you move, not to have you all the way. I want you to take what you want and give me what I want. Hard. Fast. I want everything now."

He took her words for what they were and with an upward thrust of his hips, he lodged himself all the way inside her. She clenched around him like a velvet glove, a pulsing hot one. He groaned at the delicious burn spreading through him.

Hands on her hips, he pulled her up and slammed her down, and they groaned in unison. Again and again and again, until all he could feel was her—her tight sex, her soft groans, her near sobs.

"This is what you denied me last time?" she demanded. "I should kill you!"

He laughed and they were kissing again, and slowly she caught on to his rhythm. She scraped her nails over his shoulders, her breath coming through in soft pants.

"Tell me what you need, *agapi*," he said, pressing his mouth to her long neck. Feeling her pulse between his lips. "What shall I do to push you over?"

"I don't know, Xander, everything feels too good. Don't stop moving." Then with an artless abandon, she brought his hand to her clit. When he pinched it between his fingers and rubbed, she threw her head back and clenched him harder with her sex.

Xander let her set the pace, drinking in the voluptuous picture she made. He upped the pace of his fingers and when she made those sounds that told him she was close, he nipped at her nipple. She fell apart with a soft scream he wanted no one else to hear and then he flipped her over, until her back hit the lounger and he took what he wanted from her.

He pounded into her, urgent need licking a flame through him, and when his climax came, it was with an abandon he'd never known, with a depth of feeling that mocked all of his strategies and his plans.

Within minutes, her damp flesh turned cold. Xander gathered her to him, wishing he could tell her with words how incredible it had been.

"That was…amazing," she said, sounding awed. "Was it for you too? Or is it always like this?"

"It's never like this," he said, clearing his throat. "Chemistry is inexplicable."

"Oh, good. I did okay?"

He tightened his arms around her, wondering how he'd never seen the self-doubt and the vulnerability in her before. How had he been so blind? "You were better than okay. I've never had sex out of a bed—forget out in the open, by a pool, where anyone can see us. You drive me… insane, Ani."

She giggled suddenly and he wanted to know why. He wanted to know everything about her. "OMG, I can't wait to tell Sebastian what we did to his lounger, by his pool. For once, I can shock the pants off him and not the other way and—"

He covered her mouth with his hand. "I'd prefer it if you didn't remember my brother when you're naked in my arms. Or share details about us with him."

"Are you jealous, Xander?"

"About the ease he has with you, about the affection in your words when you speak of him, yes." He marveled at how easily the admission came. Wondered if it could truly be that simple, at least, on the surface. "I've always been jealous of the hold he has on you."

"He's like a brother to me, Xander."

"A brother you would've married."

"That was an arrangement."

"That could have led to—"

"*No.* I wouldn't have slept with Sebastian. I know you don't get it, but that's not how this works. That's not how any of this works."

Silence descended between them, full of her anger and his lingering doubts. He didn't know how to tell her that it wasn't her he doubted. It was his own flaws. He would always be jealous of whatever she shared with Sebastian because he wanted it.

He wanted all of whatever she had to give. Every smile, every word, every hug, every kiss, every little piece of her vulnerable, generous heart.

"Let's go in. You need a shower."

"I can't move."

"I'll carry you."

"Can we stay here? Please? For two minutes?"

He didn't miss the wariness in her voice. Standing up, he straightened his clothes, grabbed a washcloth and ducked into the shower stall. Leaning one knee on the lounger, he gently nudged her knees open and patted her down with the washcloth.

"Thank you."

He pressed a kiss to her shoulder in reply, settling himself back against her. It was strangely disquieting how easily the intimacy came and how much he craved it. For her part, Annika didn't seem even a little surprised by it.

"Your mother's ring…" she said, a sudden clarity to her voice. "I've left it on your nightstand. I'd apologize for taking it but it wouldn't be honest."

Xander stilled behind her. For weeks he'd wanted to bring up that ring. But whatever outrage he'd nursed against her had fizzled away, leaving only curiosity. "Why did you take it?"

"I stole a few things from the first man Niven forced me to get engaged to. A family heirloom, his sister's expensive bag, a bottle of expensive drugs… It was a way to make them dislike me, to break off the agreement. The next summer, when I visited, you wouldn't look me in the eye. I mean, we were never friends like Sebastian and me, but suddenly you acted like I was dirt."

"Ani—"

"I thought, he loathes me anyway, so let me steal something from him."

"Why the ring?"

"It was the one thing you cherished. I hated the thought that you'd give it to Diana. I hated that you…pushed me to the margins of your life. I wanted to take something from you that held your heart."

Shock punched through his chest, as if someone had defibrillated his heart to wake him up. *"Annika…"* he said, an admonishment and an entreaty rolled into that single word.

"I know what I'm saying, Xander," she said, patting him on the arm as if to soothe him. "I knew your kindness even when all you showed the world was your ruthlessness."

"I do not know whether you are foolish or brave."

"A little of both? You gave me something I've never had."

He whispered something in her ear and she laughed and slapped his arm. Eyes twinkling, she looked over her shoulder at him. "That too, yes. And it was very…mighty and grand and big and thick and—"

"Minx," he said, taking her mouth in a hard, deep kiss that had them wriggling against each other like teenagers in a car.

"Shall I tell you a secret," she whispered against his lips, taunting him, "or keep it to myself forever?"

It felt as if the entire foundation of his life hung on the answer to her question.

Turning back, she nuzzled her back into his chest, and he held her to him, as he'd never done with another soul. "I think I'll hold on to it."

No words had ever made Xander feel such relief and yet such devastating loss.

As incredible as it sounded, Ani and Xander had been married for four months. He still traveled a lot and Ani practiced her cello, and when he invited her to join him for a business dinner or a charity gala or a networking event, she flew to him.

In the last month alone, she'd joined him in Tokyo, Jakarta and Paris. He never let her stay more than one night. They attended whatever important meeting he wanted her to be at, had mind-blowing sex when they returned to their hotel suite and usually he was gone when she woke up the next morning. A scribbled note would be waiting for her.

See you at home, Ani.

Ani had stashed all seven notes written in his hand on the most luxurious stationery from beautiful historical hotels in her keepsake box. It was as if she and Xander were marking a trail of their journey toward each other on the map. As if every city and hotel was standing witness to them. Apparently, beneath all the practicality she'd drilled into herself, she was an incurable romantic.

They had met her stepbrother, Niven, at the Plaza in New York on one such business trip. She'd almost begged Xander not to taint it with that meeting but in the end she had kept silent. With a perceptiveness that still amazed her, Xander had known how disturbed she'd be at the sight of the man who'd tormented her with his mind games.

For the first time in her life, Annika hadn't come away

from the meeting wanting to throw up or scratch her nails down Niven's face. Xander hadn't said one threatening word to him. In fact, he'd been downright polite. But Ani had seen the ripples in the power dynamic, had seen Niven realize that he was now facing a much bigger predator.

Then, to her shock, Xander had spent the rest of the afternoon with her and her brothers, throwing a ball and chasing their dog in Central Park. As if he'd known that Ani had needed to shed the fear and disgust from the two hours she'd spent in Niven's company.

She realized how wrong she'd been to think that he and Niven were cut from the same cloth. Not when Killian had confirmed that Xander had already set things in order to personally invest in Killian's business, to give it a boost after the malicious losses of the recent years. She'd buried the truth to protect herself.

All of Xander's actions in the last few months felt personal and her foolish heart equated it to an emotion that she was yet to see enter his eyes or fall from his lips.

She didn't push for fear of fracturing the little they had. It was an intense physical connection and a strange sort of friendship, maybe even a deep understanding of the past that had shaped them. And a commitment to their own goals. It was a strange but satisfying mishmash of things that she wasn't sure were enough to make a relationship last.

But the funny thing was that she was happy. She wanted to see where they'd go from there, if time would deepen the fragile bond that was forming between them despite themselves.

In moments of utter madness, she even found herself

hoping that Niven's diabolical mind would come up with some fresh strategy to prolong the delay in releasing her trust fund so that she could stay married to Xander.

CHAPTER TWELVE

THE PRODIGAL GRANDSON returned to the villa one bright July morning as Ani breakfasted with Xander and Thea in the front gardens. Sebastian appeared out of thin air, strolling down the cliffside toward their table, looking as dashing and handsome as ever.

Ani stared, shocked at how different he suddenly seemed. There were a million little details that differentiated him from Xander, and then there was how her heart could be so easy and light with Sebastian whereas with Xander, everything she felt was deeper, brighter, fuller.

Sebastian smiled more, though it was fake. He had a languid ease to his movements that was also fake. Then there was that perpetual mockery that filled his gray eyes.

And through her cataloging, Ani could feel Xander's gaze on her, drinking in her reaction to his twin. She didn't dare meet it, afraid of what he'd see in hers. Pursing her mouth, she picked up her coffee cup and took a sip while Sebastian kissed Thea's cheek with an effusiveness that made the older woman blush, and then gave a nod to Xander.

When Sebastian bent toward her, she pushed her chair away and shot to her feet, terrified that he'd see straight into her heart and declare in his usual mischievous way that she'd finally fallen in love.

She stumbled as the realization hit her with the force of a well-placed punch.

Xander had been relentlessly kind to her for the last two months and kindness always confused her, for she was a stranger to it. He catered to her deepest wishes, and any woman—especially one like her who had never had a real boyfriend or a real relationship—would be drawn in by his attentions. As for the sex, it was phenomenal, but that was chemistry and Xander was a man who never did anything less than perfectly. Didn't mean she was in love with him, did it?

"Still angry?" Sebastian asked, approaching her slowly.

She folded her arms. "You didn't even have the decency to send me a text, you brute."

"But I sent the next best thing. Or should I say, I sent someone better than even me?"

Ani's mouth twitched but she was damned if she would forgive the rogue so easily. "Tell me you weren't rolling around in some woman's bed and I'll forgive you."

He opened his mouth and closed it.

Outraged, she threw a filthy curse at him in Greek—one he'd taught her—and marched away.

He chased her.

Ani ran.

Sebastian ran.

Ani sped up.

He caught her and threw her over his shoulder like he used to when she was a bony ten-year-old forever following him around, and ran like a madman in circles until her head was swimming and she didn't know what was up or down. "Let me go, you brute!" she screamed, half laughing, half sobbing.

He stilled, laughing. Over his shoulder, he watched her face. "You look like you've been thoroughly and frequently sexed up. It's a good look on you."

Ani gasped and pounded his back with her fists. "You're such a—"

"I think the lady doth protest too much."

"Don't, Sebastian."

"Don't observe that you're practically glowing and while that might be because of frequent good sex, it might be because you're deliriously happy?"

"All that...don't. No games, please. Not with me. Not with him." Her heart crawled into her throat and it wasn't just because of gravity. She couldn't bear it if something Sebastian said fractured the fragile thing between her and Xander. And for all Sebastian had been her only true friend for so long, this was too private, too...precious for her to talk about. "All this is...temporary, mutually beneficial."

"Is it?"

"Yes. I'm having fun, Sebastian. Isn't that what you're always recommending? Live like a twenty-three-year-old? Sow my wild oats? Don't take life so seriously?"

"That's all you want?"

She nodded, burying every fragile wish and hope beneath a false smile. She didn't want either Thea or Sebastian interfering, playing her advocate, and somehow either guilting or arguing Xander into making this permanent. She wanted Xander to want her for herself. She wanted him to want to spend the rest of his life with her because he couldn't live without her.

Sebastian looked almost disappointed. Though that was momentary. "I guess this fairy godmother only brought you good sex, then?"

Firm, strong hands plucked her off Sebastian's shoulder before she could respond. Ani would know the touch in her sleep. Her feet hit the ground, even as half of her clung to Xander's side. She hid her very revealing blush in his chest, loving his possessive hold of her. "Enough, Sebastian. She has a bruise on her thigh that you will disturb if you throw her around like a bag of sugar."

Sebastian watched them, brows raised, not missing anything. "Your wife is no fragile flower."

"She's *my* wife, though. And I would thank you to—"

"She was my friend first. My rights trump yours."

Xander stilled next to her, a sudden tension clamping down on him, and it translated to her immediately. She wished she didn't know him so well, but she did. In his tension, in his hesitation, she saw his vulnerability. His reluctance to claim her, even in front of his twin. His inability to commit to this, even as a joke.

And her heart broke a little for him and for herself.

Ducking under his arm, she slipped out of his grasp. "I'm not going to be the bone you fight over."

Her knees were shaking under her as she returned to Thea, wondering if being in love with him meant the little she did have of him would never be enough.

Thea surprised them ten days later with an impromptu party. Ani and Xander had refused one multiple times, tired of the social circuit they'd been on for almost three months. But Thea had warmed to her and Xander together so much that she had apologized to Ani for interfering in her life, which only made Ani feel doubly guilty and desperate to confide in Thea that she'd truly fallen in love. Except Ani thought Thea already knew it. Sebastian knew it too. Killian had taken to teasing her on the phone. Even her teenage brother Ayaan knew it.

Only Xander didn't, and she so desperately wanted to tell him, but the thought of losing what little they did have stopped her.

At the announcement of a party, Ani dressed hurriedly in a floral white summer dress that clung to her breasts, put her hair into a loose side braid and perched a flower on the side. When she'd rifled through her drawer looking for a missing tube of lipstick, she found a small green velvet box under her pajamas.

Annika rubbed the soft nap of the box, her heart progressively inching into her throat. She flicked the lid open with her thumb and tears filled her eyes.

It was Xander's mother's ring, a sapphire set in yellow gold, the one she'd returned to him. The foolish, hopelessly in love part of her wanted to put it on. But he hadn't given it to her, had he?

He'd simply slipped it into her clothes drawer and the gesture—or the lack thereof—wasn't lost on her. If she wasn't careful, she'd spend the rest of her life desperately looking for hidden meaning in Xander's actions when there was none.

She arrived downstairs, flustered and hurt, to find Xander waiting for her at the foot of the stairs. He took her hand and it was clear he'd wanted to see his mother's ring on her finger. But before Ani had a chance to demand that he give it to her, Thea beckoned them.

Cousins and family friends and aunts and uncles, most of whom she'd met a few times, greeted her with an extra dose of exuberance that made Ani frown. In the midst of it all, Thea dropped her bombshell, with less pomp and circumstance than Ani would have expected, especially after all the hoops she'd insisted Xander jump through: she announced to the stunned company that she had nominated him as the chairman of Skalas Bank, effective immediately.

Suddenly, Ani understood the deference that was being offered to her. Because she was Alexandros Skalas's wife, the future Skalas matriarch, the woman who could wield as much power as Xander himself could, with their own individual fortunes.

That night, Xander didn't come to bed for a long time. The last she'd seen him, he'd been deep in talk with Thea, so Ani had bidden a thoughtful-looking Sebastian goodnight and retired.

Now, having woken up and reached for Xander, she found the bed cold. She was debating if she should go looking for him when she heard the bathroom door open. Right on cue, the shower turned on. Grabbing Xander's pillow, she nuzzled her face into it, chasing his scent.

Just thinking of how he moved inside her, how many times he'd pushed her over, made Ani's body thrum with instant need. Feeling hot under the sheets, she threw them off. Her mind turned back to the evening.

She'd congratulated Xander on his victory, as surprised as he seemed to have been. Clearly, Thea had kept it to herself until the last minute. But Annika hadn't been quite able to parse his mood out. He'd been…less than happy, if that word could be applied to Xander, ever.

Not that any of his family or cousins could read his mood. To them, he was the juggernaut behind Skalas Bank, and he would remain so for their lifetimes, ensuring their stock options and their children's trust funds stayed fat and prosperous.

She knew Sebastian had noticed Xander's strange mood. He'd even probed her for the cause, but for the first time in her life, Annika had avoided her friend's gaze. Whatever troubled Xander, she didn't want to discuss it with his twin. She felt protective about her husband, which just proved how ridiculous all of these feelings were.

Being in love with Xander was a high and a low and every crazy in between.

Her heart gave a mighty thump like it always did when he came to bed. After all these weeks, she still wasn't quite used to sharing it with him. To having him right there if she extended her arm. To find him pulling her to him in sleep, wrapping his arms and legs around her as if she were his favorite soft toy. To be woken up at all times of the night by his soft whispers and sweet caresses and, sometimes, filthy demands.

If he was insatiable with her, she was even more so with him. Her hunger for him seemed to have no end or bottom, forever filled with an urgency and fear that it might be over soon.

"I am sorry I disturbed your sleep," Xander said in a rough voice.

Ani turned and looked up.

Dressed in gray sweatpants, his chest still damp from his shower, he was watching her. With the moon hiding behind clouds, Ani couldn't make out his expression.

"I—" she licked her lips, feeling his gaze there "—reached out for you. Your side of the bed was cold and that woke me up." Cheek cradled in her palm, she exhaled. "I have gotten used to sleeping by your side. I don't like waking up alone."

His fingers came into her hair, though he made no other move to join her. Ani closed her eyes and sighed as he sifted the strands. "That is not a good idea, Annika. There is a lot more traveling in my future."

He said it easily, in his usual matter-of-fact tone, but Ani heard something else in those few words. A warning. A rebuke. A…hesitation.

But she wasn't ready for this bubble around them to break, for reality to intrude, for all of the conditions and deals they'd made to poison this sweetness. And from that fear came anger. Her spine always came back up when she was pushed. "If nothing else, it's something to put on a future dating profile—Annika Saxena-Mackenzie-Skalas likes sex and cuddling."

The night lamp came on and he moved to block its glare from falling in her eyes. She didn't know what to make of this man who protected her from everyone and everything and who gave her everything except the thing she wanted most. "That mouth needs to be punished."

Desire trickled down her spine like melted honey as images and ideas scrambled her brain. She pushed up to her elbow. The flimsy strap of her silk negligee slipped down, baring the tops of her breasts. His gaze feasted on her, and her own went to where his arousal was now clearly outlined.

And while he watched her like a hawk, Ani ran her thumb over her lower lip and then traced the shape of his erection. "Punishment…reward, *po-tay-to…po-tah-to*," she said, inching upward on the bed toward him until her mouth was near his thigh. "I think the secret to a long, happy marriage is calling it whatever the hell you want it in your head."

He grinned, his pupils already blowing out the grays. "Is that what you want, Ani? A long, happy marriage?"

Ani didn't answer. Instead, she slowly tugged the band of his sweatpants down until her prize shot up toward her. Pushing her hair away, she fisted his hard length and felt the answering dampness at her folds.

Xander stood unmoving but the grunt that fell from his mouth sounded savage in the pregnant silence.

Bracing herself on one elbow, Ani fisted him up and down, just the way he liked. That bloodthirsty streak she had observed in herself when it came to him flowed through her again. She knew his likes and wants and what could break through his ironclad control; maybe she even knew what was in his heart. "I thought men loved blow jobs. How come you've never asked me to do this?"

Lust etched into his features so that Xander looked stark, almost forbidding. He clasped her cheek with a reverent tenderness that threatened to unravel her one last secret. "I wanted it to be your choice."

"I want to go down on you. I want to blow your mind. Will you show me how to make it good? And I don't want any of your gentle bullshit. I want you to use me and my mouth however you need to get off." She licked the soft tip and looked up again. His breath was a sibilant hiss, a melody to her ears. "I want your...destruction."

He cursed. "I can't bear to hurt you, *agapi mou*."

"You won't. You'd never, Xander." She opened her mouth and closed it over the head of his shaft, and made a humming sound.

Fingers descended into her hair, and his hips thrust forward jerkily, and she realized he was trying to control himself even now. It lit a fire under her. Moving her hand from base to tip, Ani took a little more of him on the second try. This time, she felt his fingers in her hair, pressing in time with his thrust, a curse ringing out from his mouth, over and over again.

She planted her other hand on his abdomen for purchase and felt the clenched throb of his muscles there. On one exhale, she tapped his hard length against her lips and felt his full-body shudder.

"Damn, Ani. How did you—"

"I watched some stuff to see how to do it. Is it working?"

Ani took his curse as assent and continued. Her jaw ached and her core ached and she continued anyway because she wanted Alexandros Skalas undone at her hands, at her mouth. For a while, his thrusts turned rougher and jerky before he pulled out of her mouth.

She wiped the saliva from the corner of her mouth, and pushed her hair out of her face. Raking her nails over his abdomen, she held him there. "I want you to finish. In my mouth. I want—"

Leaning down, he kissed her, swallowing away her protest. "Shh, wildcat. I've used you roughly enough for your first time," he said, his voice a warning.

"But I want you to—"

He kissed her cheek and then her temple, his hard length wedged against her belly in a rough brand. Then he pushed her back onto the bed and covered her with his hard body, just the way she liked it. "Shall I do what I want with you, Ani? Shall I go harder, Ani? Take you faster? Ruin you for anyone else?"

For just a fraction of a second, Ani didn't respond. For

one thing, it was impossible to respond when her entire body was a mass of sensations with Xander pinning her with his hips and doing that thing that made her eyes roll back. For another, his question had a savage edge to it that she both loved and hated. Loved because she wanted him to see her as an equal here, needed it; hated because, even in the midst of pleasure spiraling through her, she didn't misunderstand the portent of something in his words.

Her hesitation lasted only another breath.

The stubborn, ruthless man that he was, he made her climax twice for all the "hard work" she'd put in with him. Her pleasure had been so drawn out, so acute that she thought she might have blanked out for a few seconds.

Skin damp and muscles trembling, lungs fighting for breath, Ani fell back against the bed. Xander followed her until his entire weight covered her.

Throwing her arms around his sleekly muscled back, Ani sighed in bliss. She loved it when he gave her this— all of him. Loved being pushed into the mattress by his weight. Loved fighting for breath under his broad chest. Loved when he enveloped her until her world was nothing but him and how he looked at her. Loved it when words trembled on her lips, begging to be released.

She shuddered with the effort to contain them.

Xander rolled away, taking her with him. Ani scooted closer until her back was plastered to his chest and she could hear his thundering heartbeat. His mouth was at her shoulder and his arms held her tightly.

They stayed like that for a long while and it was the happiest Annika had ever been in her life. This was it, her dream of all dreams. And she wanted to hang on to it, wanted to nurture it and build a future on it.

When she looked back at him, a wary shutter fell over his eyes instantly. She swallowed, and rubbed her nose against the bicep he'd curled around her neck. He was damp and sticky and she loved his scent in these moments. "You're in a strange mood tonight."

The same tension she'd seen in him the last few days—ever since Sebastian's return—thrummed through his body. She felt his mouth over her shoulder, his fingers drawing invisible lines on her hip. "I do not have strange moods."

"I prefer your blistering honesty, Xander. That way I always know where I stand with you."

"And you want to know where you stand with me, *agapi*? Does it make you anxious?"

"Yes, well, turns out I'm a people-pleaser in a relationship. Especially with you. After all, you're the giver of expansive, expensive gifts and I like being—" turning around, she waggled her brows suggestively "—on the receiving end."

Laughter lines crinkled out from the corners of his eyes and she wondered if he laughed more these days in general or if she was imagining things the way she wanted them. "You don't care about those gifts, Annika. And the things you do care about—"

She pressed her mouth to his cheek, gratitude and love twining through her in an overwhelming wave. "You're taking care of those."

Something serious dawned in his eyes. "You should not make a habit of depending on me for everything."

Rubbing her thumb against the corner of his mouth, she said, "It's a bad habit, I know. But the thing is, no one's ever done that for me before. No one has ever made me feel like what I want matters and—"

"Ani—"

"Yes, yes, I know, Xander. You're doing all these things because you feel guilty and because you're just naturally a protector and because it's what you'd have done for any woman you'd fake-married. There, did I cover all the bases?" she said, secretly and silently begging him to refute all her claims. Wanting him to tell her that he did all those things because her happiness mattered to him.

"I am unsettled, yes," he said, sitting up against the headboard and dragging her upright until she was half over his lap, half clinging to him.

"You didn't seem happy today. You don't seem…satisfied at Thea's announcement."

He looked at her then, his gaze holding hers but keeping its secrets. "Thea apologized for stringing me along with conditions all these years for the chairmanship even though I had earned the right more than a decade ago. She told me today's announcement came about because of you."

It wasn't the answer to her question and yet Ani couldn't stop asking. "What?"

"She said you made her see how unfair she has been to me. That she'd always demanded too much of me. 'Dumping the burdens of the family and the bank and the legacy all on his head even though he is no older than Sebastian,' apparently were your exact words."

Heat kicked up her cheeks and she shrugged. "Yes, well. You know my feelings on the subject." She frowned. "You're unhappy that I interfered?"

"Of course not."

Xander pushed a hand roughly through his hair and leaned his head back, wishing for the first time in his life that he was a different man. Wishing that the mindless pleasure of a few minutes ago wasn't the last time he made love to his wife. Wishing Ani hadn't changed him, wishing he didn't see the only way left to him was to give up the one and only thing he'd truly wanted, and needed, in his life.

"Please, Xander, tell me what's going on."

He shouldn't be surprised that Ani could see into his mood so clearly either. "For the first time in my life, I have been caught unawares. For years, becoming the chairman of Skalas Bank was my sole ambition."

"And now?" Ani said, her heart in her eyes.

"Thea has decided to travel for the next two years," he said, evading her question. He didn't know the answer even if he wanted to give it to her. For so long, all he'd cared about was the bank. But now…now that he had achieved his goal, it felt empty. And his twin's probing questions of the last few days had only shaken the foundation of his entire game. And today, finally, he knew what he needed to do. Fear gripped him with its cold fingers, leaching every bit of warmth he'd taken from Ani.

"Thea didn't tell me anything about that," Ani said, straightening, reminding him that he had to tell her without hurting her.

"I found out by accident. She is adamant about traveling and will not listen to Sebastian's admonishment that she is too old." He gently rubbed a finger over her lips. "I think you have caused ripples that even you do not understand."

"Is that a good thing or a bad thing?"

"It's a thing," he said, throwing her own words back at her. And then, because he couldn't bear to do what he needed to do while she touched him, he gently untangled himself from her and shot to his feet.

"Xander? What's going on?"

"With Thea's announcement and her travel plans, and some of the things I'm trying to figure out about the conditions attached to your trust fund, it might be better if you stay with Killian in New York for a few months. That way, you're close by for any legalities regarding the trust fund."

On her knees on the bed, the straps of her negligee loose over slender shoulders, her hair a magnificent mess around her face, she looked breathtaking. Her lips trembled but fighter that she was, she pursed them. "What about Alexandros Skalas needing a wife for all the charities and society galas that Skalas Bank hosts? What if Thea takes her nomination back and—"

"She can't. It is done."

"She trusts us not to...cheat her, right? Not to make a mockery of things?"

"I think we have already done that, *pethi mou*." Coward that he was, Xander could not look at her. "Thea will understand that I don't want to leave you here alone while I travel for weeks at a time. As for the optics of our marriage, lots of high society couples live independent lives. There is no reason you should put your life on hold. Your family, your friends are in New York. You wanted to apply to music college, right? Why not get started on that?"

She laughed but there was no warmth in the sound. "You just told me not to depend on you for everything and you've already made plans for me. And music college was just me rambling."

"Why should it be?" he said, turning around. "Why should you not go after what you want, for yourself and no one else? You are far too talented not to nurture it, Ani."

"What did I do wrong, Xander?" she said, shoulders squared, ready to fight it out with him.

He took her into his arms then. She threw her arms around his waist like she used to as a child and he pressed his mouth to her hair, his entire body shaking. His heart felt like it might punch out of his chest. "You didn't do anything wrong, *agapi*. You never did. Not now. Not then. I am the one who…" The wet splash of her tears against his chest burned him. "Thea's announcement…led to us discussing other things. Things that I have never faced, things I have hidden from Sebastian. Things I have done in foolishness, like pushing you away with the flimsiest of excuses. Things I planned even last month that I…" He looked into her eyes, his hands cupping her shoulders.

"What have you hidden from Sebastian?"

"I never told him that Mama wanted to take him along when she left Konstantin. She had all his stuff tucked away and ready to go."

Her mouth flattened, and a flash of fire sparked in her eyes. "And you?"

He shook his head. "Only him."

Ani pressed a hand to her temple, her lips trembling. "How could she have… That's cruel."

Xander shrugged, as he'd always done, although this time, he knew his indifference was a lie. "There are a lot of things that I told myself didn't matter, Ani. Only to realize I'm a fool."

Suddenly, her arms went around his waist and she hid her face in his chest and he held her loosely, scared that if he tightened his hold, he'd never be able to let go. All his schemes and strategies and risks would mean nothing even if they succeeded, if he didn't have what he wanted most.

"I'll agree," Ani said, pressing her mouth to his chest, "if you swear you aren't just…retreating from this."

"I'm not," Xander said, lying through his teeth, hoping she would forgive him when she learned the truth.

"I want another wedding present if you're going to send me away," she said, nuzzling into his chest.

He laughed then and even to his ears, the sound was a little broken. He riffled his fingers through her hair, holding her tight in the circle of his arms, wondering if he would ever feel whole again. Wondering if she would give him the chance. "What would you have of me, Ani?"

Instead of asking him for anything, Ani simply kissed him and he kissed her, wondering at how doing the right thing could feel like such painful loss.

CHAPTER THIRTEEN

"I NEED YOUR HELP," Xander said, when he finally pinned his twin down. Without Thea and Annika, the villa felt like a graveyard and he'd taken to sleeping at his penthouse in Athens. Not that he got much in the way of sleep once he'd made the most terrifying decision of his life, the biggest risk he'd ever taken. Sending Ani away had felt like ripping his heart out of his chest, but somehow he'd managed it.

"Or rather help from some of your seedier associates."

Whatever he heard in Xander's tone, Sebastian swallowed his usual facile retort and studied him. "The mighty, straightforward Alexandros Skalas wants to play dirty?"

Xander shrugged. "Just some information to bring down Niven Shah. I have most of the things in place to ruin him. Only one last part is missing."

"Ani's stepbrother?"

"I'm not going to make her wait another year until she can access her trust fund. That controlling bastard has put her through enough."

Sebastian's brow cleared. "I always wished I could have done more for her."

"You should have. Or if you found yourself incapable of it, you should have come to me."

"She didn't want my interference, Xander."

"So you leave her to deal with an untenable situation alone?"

"Such sympathy for Ani when you had none for Mama? She was caught in just such a situation."

Xander felt as if his twin had slapped him. Their mother was one topic they never discussed. Never. Their parents had broken them in different ways, and while their father had been a true monster, their mother... Xander had always thought of her as weak. Thought himself and Sebastian better off without her. He was only beginning to realize that this rationalization provided himself a false comfort.

"Annika is nothing like her," Xander said, his throat feeling as if it was full of hot coals. "But it should please you to see she has made me realize how harsh I was about Mama. Not everyone can be strong like Ani. Some women break. Some women run. I don't know if I can forgive Mama ever, but I can wish that she found peace after she left us with him. I mean it," Xander said.

Sebastian swallowed and nodded.

"You should know something, though, Sebastian. Your faith in her was very much returned," he said, gathering the courage to say the words he'd buried so deep that he'd only accessed it again at the prospect of wanting a future with Ani. And knowing himself inadequate to meet it. Only now, when he'd acknowledged how much it hurt to lose Ani, how much he doubted his ability to be what she needed, he could feel this other pain too. "Mama never meant to leave you behind."

His brother stared, stunned.

"I found her traveling bag the previous night. She had

your passport and hers and your medication and your art supplies. She had every intention of taking you with her."

A curse spat out from Sebastian's mouth, as if it was poison he had to expel from his system.

"I think Konstantin discovered her plans at the last minute and she had no choice but to leave in a hurry." Xander forced himself to meet his twin's eyes. So alike and yet so different. "I am sorry I never told you that. I was…devastated that she would leave me behind with him. That she didn't think I needed her love and her protection just as much as you did."

"You left that evening and stayed with your friends," Sebastian whispered, his brow clearing. "I can't imagine what you must have felt, Xander."

"Three months ago, I would have said it was her loss." The words came easily. "I molded myself to make that true, to not need anyone ever again. But when I—" he swallowed the abject pain and misery filling his very breath "—when I realized I wanted a future with Ani, a real one, I realized what Mama's thoughtless abandonment has cost me." He was too ashamed to tell Sebastian how at first he'd strategized to win Ani's love and commitment like a game, only to realize that it would shame and taint everything she gave him and everything they shared. That in the end, she'd realize that he'd given her everything but love.

Sebastian's gaze reflected the bitter understanding of Xander's loss. "I'll get you what you need to beat Niven. You're right. It's high time Ani was free."

Xander clapped his brother on the shoulder. For the first time in their lives, that one thread of resentment that had always simmered between them died. The topic of their mother was put to rest.

"Have you told Ani that she'll have her fortune earlier than she imagined?" Sebastian asked as Xander turned to leave. "That you're ruining Niven?"

"No. It is not her burden to carry."

"Not even that you're in love with her?" Sebastian taunted with a raised brow.

Denial danced on Xander's lips but wouldn't take shape. "She should be free, Sebastian. Free to make her own choices. Free to live her life the way she wants. Free to be who she is."

If Xander thought his twin would convince him otherwise, he was wrong. Sebastian simply nodded.

For all that they were different in temperament, in this it seemed they agreed. Or maybe Konstantin was powerful and ruthless enough to cast a shadow on their lives from even beyond the grave. Because more than anything, Xander refused to bind a woman to him when she had no choice. Especially Annika, who should be free to love as she pleased.

As if he knew exactly where Xander's mind went, his twin surprised him yet again. "You're nothing like Konstantin, Alexandros," he said. "You should also know that I would not have left with Mama, not without you. Not for anything."

Xander nodded, knowing in his gut that his brother spoke the plain, unvarnished truth. Despite trying his best to pit them against each other, Konstantin hadn't broken their bond. And it was a thing he had always been glad for. Even if he'd gambled away the one thing he loved most in the world, the one person who showed him what happiness could be, and who he could be.

* * *

Annika was sitting under the covered patio in the backyard of Killian's house on a lazy Saturday, watching the boys play, when she got the first phone call from some big-shot lawyer from a fancy law firm in NYC.

It had been a month since she'd traveled to New York. She'd seen Xander only once since then. Once in five weeks and three days, to be exact. And that was only because when he'd told her that she'd have to meet Niven one more time, she'd nearly cried on the phone at the prospect.

Xander hadn't calmed her down or done anything normal like that. No, just as she'd sat down to lunch with Niven at the Plaza, he'd walked in through the doors, kissed her senseless, and spent the next three hours grilling Niven and his lawyer about the conditions for her trust fund.

Ani had spent most of that three-hour meeting daydreaming of him dragging her to his suite and ravishing her to make up for two weeks of no sex. Instead, when the meeting had finished, he'd kissed her again with such tenderness, told her he was expected in Tokyo and walked away, leaving her staring after him like a kicked puppy.

She hadn't gotten it even then.

Now she saw what he'd done, as her phone rang over and over. Thea called and congratulated her on winning a battle she'd fought for so long. Sebastian called and asked how it felt to be free, and an heiress. Niven called and while Ani had barely said anything on the phone, he'd yelled and begged her to stop her damned husband because he was ruining Niven.

Ani fell back against her lounger, shock buffeting her this way and that.

Xander had not only strong-armed Niven into releasing her trust fund months—probably years—ahead of schedule, but he was also destroying ruining him for his sins against her. And he hadn't said a whisper of any of it to her.

"No one will make you do anything you do not want to do ever again," he'd said, cradling her against his chest at the helipad. *"Not Thea, not Killian. Not even me."*

Only now did she understand that he'd released her from their agreement. Because he'd received the coveted chairmanship of Skalas Bank? Because he didn't need the farce anymore? Because her usefulness as the socialite Skalas wife was done?

No, the man she loved was not that cruel, that ruthless, that calculating. Not with her. Was it because he didn't, couldn't, love her? Because he found it easy enough to leave her, like her mother had?

Annika swiped her phone on and her trembling fingers hovered on the call log. Could she sound coherent if she heard his voice on the other end? Could she not beg him to take her back? Could she not blurt out that after everything he'd won for her—her fortune, her revenge, her ability to say goodbye to a battle that had cost her too much—she'd lost the most important thing?

In the end, she chickened out and typed a text instead.

They're saying the trust fund is mine. What should I do?

His reply came back within a minute.

Nothing for you to do. All the legalities will be taken care of. Enjoy it.

What does it mean, Xander?

This time, his reply took forever—or at least the three minutes felt like forever, and the entire time her heart thudded so loudly in her chest that she couldn't hear anything beyond its wild thrashing.

It means you are free, Ani. Of duties and obligations and battles and wounds. Free to begin a new life, free of controlling men. Free to pursue your dreams, whatever they might be. As you should be, agapi.

Annika laughed because it was probably the longest and most grammatically correct text in the history of texting and then she was sobbing because Xander was giving her up and it felt like her heart was breaking into so many shards. He'd given her her freedom and her fortune—everything she'd ever wanted—and still somehow managed to cheat her.

The phone slipped from her hand to the ground with a soft thunk. She pulled her legs up to her chest because it hurt everywhere and she felt as if she was drowning, and even the boys running up to her, anxious and scared and angry and a little heartbroken, wouldn't stop the tide of tears pulling her under.

Because she wanted him—Alexandros Skalas. And he'd told her while calling her his love that he would not give her his heart.

CHAPTER FOURTEEN

The sun was painting the horizon over the Ionian Sea a decadent splash of pinks and oranges when Annika walked into the first floor of the Villa Skalas on a bright December evening, six and a half months after Xander had sent her away.

Three months after he'd turned her into an heiress and yet robbed her of the one thing she'd held precious. Despite never wanting to step foot in the villa again, she'd taken the first flight Sebastian had booked for her without asking questions.

The first floor was ominously empty and she wondered if something terrible had happened to her godmother, if she was too late. The last time she'd spoken to her, Thea had been in Morocco, but admitted, when Annika had relentlessly badgered her, that she had developed a bout of pneumonia. Ani had instantly told Sebastian. That was three weeks ago. When he'd told her two days ago that Thea was worse, Ani had begged to come home to the villa.

Her heart raced. The entire villa seemed to be empty. She plucked her cell phone out of her bag and was scrolling through it when a tall shadow emerged from the terrace.

Relief and fear warred in her as Ani took a step forward. "Sebastian? How is she? Where is she? Can we go to the hospital immediately?"

The tall shadow took a few more steps further in and she realized her mistake.

It was *not* Sebastian, once again.

It was the man who had broken her heart as easily and effortlessly as he'd once stepped up to marry her.

It was Xander, looking like he'd been dragged under a bus. He had dark shadows under his eyes, his hair was too long and curled around his ears, and his white shirt fell loosely against his lean chest, as if he hadn't been... No, she was not going there.

"What the hell are you doing here?" she said, unable to rein in her temper. Anger had always been her refuge when she was hurt. "Where's Thea?"

He raised his hands, palms facing her as if asking for forgiveness. "Thea is well. I mean, she is still recovering from pneumonia, but she's not as serious as Sebastian led you to believe. She's given up traveling for now and is resting, which is what she needs."

"What do you...?" Ani swallowed and fought the urge to step back as Xander moved forward. "Then why?"

"She *has* been in really bad shape. We didn't tell you for a while because I...didn't want to worry you."

"Because you're the lord and master of everything, right? You get to decide what's right for everyone?" she bit out.

"No, Ani. I'm trying not to be that person. But it's a lifetime's habit."

She tapped her feet impatiently, hiding her shock at his raw admission. "And now?"

"She has been asking for you."

Annika glared at him. "But Sebastian made it sound worse. What the hell is wrong with you both?" She grabbed her bag and turned around, intent on walking all the way to the nearest village if that was what it took to get away from him.

"He didn't want to but I twisted his arm."

Annika's steps faltered at Xander's admission, but she kept trying to put one foot in front of the other. Granted, she didn't cover the entire damn distance to the double doors that opened out into the courtyard, but she was halfway there. Even if her stupid legs and her stupid heart refused to listen to sense.

"Aren't you curious why?"

Ani hesitated, then turned around. As long as she didn't let him touch her or kiss her, she would get away. She would not fall for his comforting lies again. Folding her arms—to hide their shaking more than anything else—she tipped her chin up. "Fine. Why?" she said, using her most bored tone ever. It was gratifying to know that she could still pull it off.

"Why did you ask him for a loan?"

"None of your business. And since Sebastian apparently cannot keep a secret from you, you can tell him I have no use for his money anymore. In fact, tell him I'm done with him too. I've had enough of you both manipulating me."

That her hit had landed was only betrayed by the flattening of his mouth. "Why did you give away your fortune after battling your stepbrother for years? After letting him control you with it for so long? What was the point?"

That was what this was about? "You were right, for once," Ani said, knowing he'd never rest if she didn't answer him. "The trust fund…became a weight from the past. I thought I'd be free if I had it, or that I would have my mother's blessing in some twisted way. That I would somehow have what should have been mine, for once. Instead, it only felt like another shackle."

"So you gave it away to your brothers and charity."

"If you know everything, why are you asking me?"

"Because I'd like to understand."

"Understand what, Xander?"

"Why didn't you at least keep enough for college?"

"Because I got my hands on it through you. You and your favors and your pity would taint any education I used it for. You would stay with me forever, even though you washed your hands off me. I wanted to be free of you too. Not just Niven. I wanted my life, my choices to be my own. Completely. Especially after I realized…how much of a shadow you could cast on my future. I couldn't be beholden to you in any way."

He flinched as if she'd slapped him, and whatever satisfaction Ani had imagined getting out of telling him never materialized. In fact, she only felt an overwhelming sense of loss all over again.

"You're very stubborn and determined, aren't you?" he said, staring at her as if he was seeing her for the first time.

"Not a single phone call, not a text for six freaking months and you've the gall to question me now."

"What do you plan to do now?"

God, the man was relentless. Ani sighed. "I plan to go to college. Which is why I asked Sebastian for a loan. I plan to sleep my way through a thousand guys in college. I plan to live and laugh and make choices that have nothing to do with the past. I plan to live for me. And I plan to live it out of the shadow of the man who made me realize that I had my freedom all along, to make the choices I wanted. I just had to grasp it."

"That is all I wanted for you, Ani," he said, somehow reaching her.

Suddenly, he was close. So close that she could breathe in his cologne and sweat. Could see the swirling storm that deepened his gray eyes. Could see the tension radiating from him as if someone was holding him down and he was thrashing to break free. "The freedom to make a choice."

Tears ran down Annika's face with no warning. Something about his words unlocked the tight hold she'd kept on herself for months. She wiped them roughly with the back of her hand. "You didn't even have the decency to tell me that you're dumping me the moment you had your chairmanship."

"Is that what you think, *agapi*? That I dumped you because I had no more use for you?"

"Your actions speak for you, Xander. And even this…" she ran a hand between them both "…you manipulated this. You couldn't see me in New York?"

"I wanted you home, Ani. I wanted the best advantage. I wanted—"

"What the hell are you talking about?" Ani said, pushing at his chest as he crowded her, beyond incensed now.

"I wanted to be your choice, *pethi mou*. I didn't want you to be mine because you had no choice. Because you needed a husband for that trust fund. Because I was your first or because you are attached to this damned villa and Thea and Sebastian or because I helped you achieve that freedom. I wanted to be your choice when all you had were choices and freedom and fortune and your entire life ahead. I needed to be your choice. Because you're mine, Ani. I knew that, long before I made love to you. I knew, I think, that night at the ballroom, when I first heard you play the cello."

* * *

She looked at him as if he was spinning impossible and incredible stories out of nothing. Xander felt her disbelief like a gash in his skin and that was his own fault.

"You didn't even touch me for weeks after the gala. You lavished me with gifts and the boys' visit and…if you knew you wanted me, for real, forever, you couldn't have waited. You couldn't have kept me at a distance. You don't know what love is if you can do that, Xander."

He rubbed a hand over his face, every accusation hitting him where it hurt the most. "I knew, Ani. I knew and I sat with the truth. I knew and I strategized, calculated the risk, forecasted the outcome. I…planned to bind you to me through any number of means. I—"

"You're a ruthless bastard."

"I am, *agapi*. I knew I couldn't let you go. And I did everything except consider the possibility of loving you. Of telling you what you meant to me. Of telling you that you showed me the shape of a future I couldn't live without."

She pressed a hand to her mouth but her soft cry had already escaped. Eyes big in her angular face, she stared at him with anger and pain and so much love that Xander thought it might shatter him to pieces.

"Before Thea made that announcement, you were so happy with me. Then Sebastian returned and he asked me what I was doing to you and I knew that it was wrong. That it wasn't enough. That night, after the party, I told you that Thea and I talked. I realized how much I…loved you, how I was afraid to tell you that, how I hated the fact that you were mine because you had no choice. I loved you so much that it hurt. I shuddered at the thought of you finding me inadequate. Of failing you. Of losing you before I even had you. I went in circles until I knew what I had to do."

"You manipulated me, spun sweet lies in my ears, and sent me away because you loved me?" she said, throwing the words at him now. Tears running down her cheeks. "You still don't know what it means to love, Xander."

"I do, *agapi mou*. You taught me what it is," Xander said, covering the last distance between them. "Then and now. I love you so much, Ani, that it—"

"I hate you," Ani yelled, when he clasped her cheeks and pressed a gentle, reverent kiss to her temple. "For six months, every day, I waited for a text, a call. Every day, I waited for one of your fancy lawyers to serve me divorce papers. Every day, I called Sebastian and tried to ask him where you were, with whom, if you had—" She broke as a sob rose through her, and his arms were around her and it was the only place in the world she ever wanted to be.

"I hate you," she whispered again, and suddenly she was airborne as he was carrying her and running up two stories with her cradled in his arms, whispering rapidly enough in Greek that she couldn't half hear his words, and then he was placing her in his bed, *their* bed, and kneeling between her legs which she had automatically parted for him. And then he was kissing her.

Xander was kissing her and Ani didn't care if the universe itself had caved in in that moment.

Roping her arms around his neck, she shamelessly threw herself into the kiss. It was more necessary than air and it was sloppy and messy because she was still crying and then she bit his lower lip because she was so…angry.

"Every day of the last six months has been an eternity," Xander whispered, dragging out a long kiss. His hands and his mouth were everywhere and nowhere enough. "Ayaan told me you were going to parties, dances, nightclubs. Every time he told me you went out with someone again, a piece of my heart was chipped away. But I told myself that's what you needed. That I had to wait. That even if you went to some other man, all that would matter was that you returned to me. It was torment of the worst kind."

Ani stared up at him, feeling his pain as her own. "You're way too possessive to even imagine me going to another man, Xander."

"I hoped that you wouldn't, *agapi*. But I had to prepare for the worst."

"And if I had, Xander? If I had fallen in love with someone else?"

He took her hand and pressed his face into her palm, tension wreathing his lean frame. "It's strange, isn't it? The kind of conviction you have in your gut when you love someone? I had this…faith—which felt irrational enough at times—that you loved me too. That you would return to me eventually."

"So you tormented us both in the process?" Ani said, rubbing her thumbs over the shadows under his eyes. "I had no idea you and Ayaan were in touch."

"The little fiend is as cunning as Sebastian. He's been texting me with enough details to write a book."

Laughter broke out of her. "Hey, that's my little brother."

"Well, he is a little rascal."

"He knew how much I cried every night. He kept bringing me ice cream. He knew I was pining over you, and all the time you were keeping track of me and he never told either of us."

Xander smiled, feeling as if his heart was beating in his

chest again. "You look happy at the thought of me being tormented, *agapi*."

Her brown eyes shone like precious gems, one lone tear still running down her cheek. "I'm bloodthirsty enough to like it. Xander, how could you—"

"Because I love you, Kyria Skalas. I know how much you hate Niven. I know how my father tormented my mother with his need to control and dominate and take away her choices. I... I love you so much that I had to let you go. When Sebastian told me you asked for a loan, I had my lawyers poke into Killian's affairs. He told me what you'd done, against his objections. For the first time in months, I took a full breath. It felt like a sign. And then, Ayaan told me you...haven't been happy for a single day since I sent you back. And I couldn't bear to be away from you any longer. Thea is desperate to see you. And I am desperate for you to stay."

"Xander—"

"Be mine, Ani," he said, pressing his face into her chest, asking for a benediction. "Give me a chance to make all those dreams of yours real. Build a life with me. Build a family with me."

Ani plastered herself to his chest, wrapping her arms around his broad back. She was still trembling, a scared part of her wondering if this was all a sweet dream from which she would be torn at dawn. "You are mine, Xander."

"Marry me again. Just for you and me. Marry me, Ani."

"Yes, please. But tell me again. Tell me how much you love me."

"Enough to sustain Sebastian's constant mocking. Enough to realize that for the first time in my life, I wondered if my mother's loss had left me whole. Enough to want to be a better man."

"I love you, Xander. I have loved you for as long as I can remember and when you push me out of your life, then and now—"

"I'm sorry, *agapi mou*. Even then, I was afraid, you see. I had realized too late how attached I was to you. How impossible a relationship between us could be. And the thought nearly broke me. So, in my usual way I told myself you meant nothing to me. That you didn't deserve my..." He groaned and Ani laughed. "I was the one who didn't see you, who didn't know you, who didn't deserve you, *matia mou*. But I promise I will do my best to deserve you, to have you and hold you."

"You have me, Xander," Ani said, and kissed him and dragged him on top of her.

And when he looked into her eyes she said yes once again, and he took her away to ecstasy and belonging and a forever kind of love that she'd thought only existed in her dreams.

* * * * *